Chantry could detect no move ____ _____ ____ ____ took his rifle and crossed the sparse grass to the doorway. The latch-string was out.

He went inside. It was as trim indoors as out.

The hewn planks of the ceiling lay from beam to beam, fitted tightly. There seemed to be no—

He distinctly heard the sound . . . A horse walking, a horse that came slowly forward, then paused . . . just outside.

Owen Chantry turned swiftly, rifle in hand.

The girl was facing him, wide-eyed. For a moment they stared at each other.

"You're more beautiful than I expected," he said.

BRIONNE
THE BROKEN GUN
THE BURNING HILLS
THE CALIFORNIOS
CALLAGHEN
CATLOW
CHANCY
CONAGHER
DARK CANYON
THE DAYBREAKERS
DOWN THE LONG HILLS
THE EMPTY LAND
FALLON
THE FERGUSON RIFLE
THE FIRST FAST DRAW
FLINT
GALLOWAY
GUNS OF THE TIMBERLANDS
HANGING WOMAN CREEK
THE HIGH GRADERS
HIGH LONESOME
HOW THE WEST WAS WON
THE KEY-LOCK MAN
KID RODELO
KILLOE
KILRONE
KIOWA TRAIL

LANDO
THE LONELY MEN
THE MAN CALLED NOON
THE MAN FROM THE
  BROKEN HILLS
THE MAN FROM SKIBBEREEN
MATAGORDA
MOJAVE CROSSING
MUSTANG MAN
NORTH TO THE RAILS
OVER ON THE DRY SIDE
THE QUICK AND THE DEAD
RADIGAN
REILLY'S LUCK
RIDE THE DARK TRAIL
RIVERS WEST
SACKETT
THE SACKETT BRAND
SACKETT'S LAND
SHALAKO
SILVER CANYON
SITKA
THE SKY-LINERS
TAGGART
TREASURE MOUNTAIN
TUCKER
UNDER THE SWEETWATER RIM
WAR PARTY

OVER ON THE DRY SIDE

□

Louis L'Amour

BANTAM BOOKS · TORONTO · NEW YORK · LONDON

OVER ON THE DRY SIDE
A Bantam Book

PRINTING HISTORY
*Saturday Review Press edition / October 1975
2nd printing ... December 1975
Bantam edition / May 1976*

ISBN 0-553-02452-3

Published simultaneously in the United States and Canada

*Bantam Books are published by Bantam Books, Inc. Its trade-
mark, consisting of the words "Bantam Books" and the por-
trayal of a bantam, is registered in the United States Patent
Office and in other countries. Marca Registrada. Bantam
Books, Inc., 666 Fifth Avenue, New York, New York 10019.*

PRINTED IN THE UNITED STATES OF AMERICA

To
Don Demarest,
companion
of the
High Country–

1   All that spring, I was scared. Why Pa ever took a notion to stop on that old Chantry place I never did know. Maybe it was because he was just tired and wishful of stopping someplace . . . anyplace.

There'd been a dead man on the steps by the door when we drove up. He'd been a long time dead, and nobody around to bury him, and I was scared.

The cabin was strong. It was built mighty solid like whoever had shaped it up and put it together had planned to stay. That was before the Indians come.

There was nobody inside and the place was all tore up . . . of course. It had been vacant for weeks, prob'ly. Maybe even months. That man had been dead a long time.

There wasn't much left but torn skin, dried out like

old leather, and bones. His clothes was some tore up and all bloody.

Pa, he stood there looking down at him a long time. "Don't seem logical," he said, at last.

"What's that, Pa?"

"Indians most usually take a body's clothes. They ain't taken nothin' from him."

"His pockets is inside out."

"I was seein' that, boy. It do make a body think." He turned. "Boy, you run out to the wagon an' git my shovel. We got a buryin' to see to."

He stepped around the body and pushed wide the cabin door. That door had been half-open, and Pa looked in like he feared what he might see, but like I said, there wasn't nothin' to fear.

When I come in later I saw just what he saw. A bed with two sides nailed to the outside wall, a table, two chairs . . . all mighty well made by a man with lovin' hands for wood.

Pa always said you could tell a man who loved wood by the way things were fitted and dressed, nothing halfway, but smooth and nicely done. Pa couldn't do that sort of work himself, but he had admiration for it, and it made me feel like working at it until I was good. If fine work impressed Pa so much there must be something to it.

"I never had no craft, boy. I worked hard all my life but never had no craft. Just a few slights I picked up handling heavy things and the like. I do admire a man who does fine work. It is a pleasure to look upon."

We taken that dead man out to the hill back of the house and we dug us a grave. When we'd dug it down we laid that body in a blanket, covered it around him sweet an' neat, and then we lowered him easy into the ground and Pa said a few words from the Book.

I never did know how Pa come to so much knowing of the Book, because I never did see him reading much in it.

We filled in the grave an' Pa said, "Come tomorrow we'll make him a marker."

"How'll you know what to say? We ain't sure who he is."

"No, we ain't. But they do call this the Chantry place, so I reckon his name must be that." Pa stopped there, leaning on his shovel, like.

"What'll we do now, Pa? It's late to be startin' on."

"This here's it, son. This place here. We ain't goin' no further. You know, son, I ain't been much of a success in my time. Fire burned me out back to home, and we lost everything. In Missouri the grasshoppers et it all up, and in Kansas it was hail. But you know, I never was much hand at pickin' land.

"Your grandpap, now he knowed land. He could look at what growed there, and he knew. He could ride over land at a gallop and tell you which was best, but me, I was a all-fired smart youngster and no old man was going to tell me anything. I just knowed it all already. So I never learned.

"Son, I got to admit it. Ever' piece of land I picked was poor. Sure, we lost out to grasshoppers, hail, and the like, but those places never would have made it no way.

"Now this here . . . some other man picked this. I heard talk of Chantrys and they were knowing folk. The man who built this house, he was a knowing man. He had a craft. So I reckon maybe he picked himself a right good piece of land.

3

"So this here is it. We just ain't a-goin' no further."

We cleaned out the cabin. We mopped an' we dusted like a couple of women, but she was spic an' span when we finished.

The shed and the stable were solid-built, and there were good tools in the shed, leaning just like that dead man must have left them.

Right close to the house was a spring, not more'n thirty feet away. Good cold water, too. Never tasted no better.

There was a fieldstone wall around that spring, maybe eight, ten foot back from it, so a body could get water and go back to the cabin, leaving himself open to fire only in front. Even that was partly protected by a swell of the ground.

Cabin had a good field all around, and a corral joined the house to the barn. The horses had been run off, and whatever other stock he might have had, but we pulled our wagon close and we unloaded.

Not that I liked it much. Fact was, I didn't like it at all. Ever' time we stepped out of that cabin we stepped over where that dead man had lain. I never liked that.

Pa said, "Pay it no mind, son. That man would admire to see folks usin' what he built. No man with a craft builds to throw away. He builds to use, and to last, and it would be a shameful thing to leave it die here, all alone."

"Ain't no neighbors, Pa."

"We don't need neighbors right now. We need time an' hard work. If this here land's rich as I think, neighbors will come. Only when they do they'll find a fair piece of it staked out an' marked for we 'uns."

"Maybe those Indians will come back."

He just looked at me. "Boy, your pa ain't as smart

4

as some, but I'm smart enough to know that Indians take the clothes off a dead man because they need 'em."

"His clothes wasn't taken," I said, wanting to argue with him.

"You bet. His clothes wasn't taken, but somethin' else was. You notice his pockets, boy?"

"They were inside out."

"They surely were. Now, boy, somebody wanted what was in that man's pockets. Money and the like. Indians this part of the country don't set much store by money. They want *goods*. They want *things*. Ain't no money in them wigwams."

"You mean, it wasn't Indians?"

"Seen no moccasin tracks, boy. But I seen boot tracks a-plenty. Those who killed that man weren't Indians. They was white men."

We were eatin' supper when Pa said that, and it give me a chill. If it wasn't no Indian, then we were in trouble, 'cause a man can tell an Indian. He can spot him right off. But a bad white man? How you goin' to tell until he's bad?

I said as much. Pa, he just looked at me and said, "Boy, you see strangers around, you come tell me, you hear? But you see 'em first, an' when you do you get clean out of sight."

Wasn't much time for thinkin' about things, because we worked. Seemed like Pa felt he owed something to the dead man, because he worked a sight harder than I ever seen him before. It was work from can see to cain't see, for Pa an' me.

We measured out four sections of land . . . four square miles of it, field, forest, meadow, and stream.

We had seed corn and some vegetable seeds. We planted forty acres to corn, and of an acre we made a vegetable garden. One reason we taken that corner because there was berries in it.

But I never did forget that dead man.

The stranger, when he came was alone. He was one man riding.

He was a slim, tall man with a lean, dark face and high cheekbones. He wore a black store-bought suit and a bandanna tied over his head like in the old pirate pictures. He had polished black boots, almighty dusty, and a fine black horse with a white and pink nose.

He stopped afar off, and that was when I first seen him. He stood in his saddle and shaded his eyes at us, seeing me first and then Pa, who was working with a hoe in the cornfield.

"Pa?" I said, just loud enough.

"All right, boy. I seen him."

Pa had his rifle in a scabbard set next to a bush close by. I seen him start to usin' his hoe over thataway, but this man on the black horse came right along, an' when I looked again I seen he was leading a spare . . . a packhorse. I guess it had been hidden behind him before, and I'd missed seeing it.

He come on toward the house settin' easy in the saddle, and then I seen he carried a rifle in a scabbard, too. Close to his hand. From under his coat I could see the tip end of a holster.

Pa wasn't far from the house but he moved over to stand where his rifle was, and he waited there. The man rode up, and called out, "Is it all right to get a drink? We've come far and we're almighty thirsty."

Pa taken up his rifle and walked toward the house, leaving the hoe where the rifle had been. "He'p yourself," Pa said. "It's a dusty road you've traveled."

6

The man's features relaxed a little, almost like he was going to smile, only I thought he didn't smile very much, by the look of him. "Yes, it is. Most of my roads are dusty, it seems like." He glanced around. "Is this the Chantry place?"

"They call it that."

"Are you a Chantry?"

"No. I'm not. We found the place deserted. Found a dead man on the doorstep. We buried the man, and we moved in. Seemed too fine a place to lay idle."

Pa paused a moment, and then he said, "Even if the land weren't so good, I'd have hesitated to go on. That man Chantry, if he was the one built this place, had a feelin' for good work. I just couldn't bear to see it left run down."

The man looked at Pa a long minute. "I like that," he said then, "I think Chantry would want you here."

He drank from our gourd dipper. The water was cold an' sweet. We both knew how welcome that kind of water was to a long-ridin' man.

Pa taken to him. I seen that right off. There was somethin' lonely and standoffish about that man, yet there was warmth in 'im, too. Like he had a lot of friendship in him that hadn't been used.

"Might's well stay the night," Pa said. "It's a fur piece to anywhere from here. Beyond, there's the wild country."

"Well," the man hesitated. "My horses could stand the rest. Thank you, and we will."

"You he'p him, boy," Pa said. "I'll start some bacon in the pan."

We went to the stable. I always liked that stable. In the hottest weather it was always shadowy and cool. The walls was thick, the roof was high, and there was a loft in one end for the hay we'd mow come autumn time. I like the smell of fresh-mowed hay, of horses and harness, saddles and such.

"You got some fine horses, mister," I said.

He nodded, putting a gentle hand on the black's shoulder. "Yes, I have. You can always put your trust in a good horse, son. Treat them right and they'll always stay by you."

We took the rig from his riding horse and then from the buckskin packhorse. It was a heavy load— lots of grub and a blanket roll. From the feel of the blanket roll I near 'bout decided he had another rifle or a shotgun hidden there. . . . One or t'other.

Then he commenced to work on his horses. He taken out a currycomb and he done a good job, first one, then the other.

"Been here long, son?"

"Got here early spring. We put in a crop soon as we cleaned up."

"Cleaned up? Was the place a mess?"

"Nossir. It was in mighty good shape, 'cept dusty and all. Course, it was tore up a mite inside by them men searchin'."

"Searching?"

"Them men that killed him. They tore things up like they was huntin' for somethin'." I paused, not sure how much I should say. "Pa don't think it was Indians."

"No?"

"That dead man . . . his clothes wasn't took, and his pockets was turned inside out. Pa says Indians would take his clothes . . . an' maybe burned the place."

"Your pa is right." He paused, his hands resting on the horse's back. "I like your pa, son. He seems

8

like a right-thinking man. And I think he's correct. Chantry would have wanted a man like him on the place."

Then he taken his saddlebags and rifle, an' we walked to the house with the smell of wood smoke and bacon frying. He paused there on the stoop, and looked out an' around. You could see a far piece from the door, 'cross meadows and past stands of timber. It was a pretty view, and the man just stood there, lookin' at the rose color in the clouds where the sun was leaving a memory on the sky.

"Yes," he said, "this would be the place. This was what he would have wanted."

The floor inside was clean-swept and mopped. He glanced about, and I could see approval in his eyes. Pa saw it, too.

"I never had much," he said, "but I've got sense enough to know that a place doesn't stay nice without you keep it so. It takes a deal of work to build a place, and a deal of work to keep it up."

The food was good, and Pa always made a good cup of coffee. I knew that from what folks said, for Pa never let me have coffee 'cept a couple times on mighty cold mornin's.

"Too bad about that dead man," the stranger suddenly said. "Anybody know who he was?"

"I ain't been to town but once't and never talked to nobody 'bout it more'n to just report I'd found a body and buried it. I guess nobody knew Chantry well, or much about his place.

"There ain't no sheriff. Just a marshal, and he pays no mind to nothin' outside the town. I 'spect the dead man was the Chantry the place was named for, but I got no way of knowin'. There wasn't nothin' in his pockets."

"Nothing inside the house either?"

"Only books. A lot of them books, thirty or forty. Never look at 'em m'self. I don't find much time for readin', nor the boy, either. Though he seems to have a leanin' toward it . . . like his ma. She was a reader."

Pa hesitated, then said quietly, "My wife's friends figured she married beneath her. That was one reason we come on west. Only she never made it. She died in Westport of the cholera."

"Was there anything else of his?"

"In that desk yonder. There's papers and things. They was scattered all over when we come in the place. Dust over the papers. Some blood."

Pa paused. "Y'know, mister, I never said this even to my son, but I b'lieve there was somebody here with Chantry. Somebody who either went away with whoever come and killed him. Or who was taken away or maybe left before his killer come."

The stranger looked at Pa. "You are an observing man."

Pa shrugged his thin shoulders and refilled the stranger's cup. "See that alcove yonder? With the bed in it? Well, there was another bed in t'other room, and that alcove had a curtain before it.

"The curtain was tore down when we come, but it ain't likely there'd be a curtain lest there was a woman in the house. I figger that woman either run away or was took away, and if she run away I figger she'd come back to bury her man."

"So the mystery deepens," the stranger smiled, showing even white teeth under his black mustache. "You've done some thinking."

"I have. There's a deal of time for it, with the work and all to keep a man's hands busy. But not his mind. It's by way of protection, too, for there's two ways

10

to think if they were white men. Either they come to rob him of what he had, and robbed him, or they come lookin'. For something else.

"Now if they came lookin' for something else and didn't find it, they'll be comin' back." Pa glanced at me. "I think the boy's been thinkin' of that, and it worries him."

"It is a thing to consider," the stranger said. "I think your son is wise."

"It ain't only them," I burst out of a sudden. "It's *her!*"

"Her?" The stranger looked at me.

"That girl . . . that . . . woman! If she comes back, this place is hers. All Pa's work'll be for nothin'."

"If she returns," the stranger replied, "I think she would be pleased that her friend had been buried and the place cared for. I should believe she would be very grateful, indeed.

"I cannot presume to speak for her, but do you stay on without fear and, if she returns, you will find you have lost nothing and perhaps gained much."

"They didn't get her," I said then. "She got away."

Pa looked at me, surprised. The stranger stopped with his fork halfway to his mouth. Slowly, he lowered it. "How can you know that?"

"I seen tracks out back. They were old tracks, but a body could read 'em. Somebody came up, ridin' easy . . . cantering. Of a sudden that horse was pulled up awful sharp, his hoofs dug in an' he reared, then that horse turned in his own tracks and took off like lightnin' for the hills."

"Did you see any other tracks?"

"Yessir. They taken out after her. There was two, three of 'em . . . maybe four. But she had a good horse an' a good lead."

11

"They still might have caught her."

"They never done it. She got into them hills, and she knowed them hills like her own hands. She . . ."

"How d'you know that?" Pa said.

"The way she taken to them hills, no stoppin', no hesitatin' like. She rode right into them hills and she got to the little valley yonder an' when she got there she drove a bunch of cattle—"

"What cattle?" Pa said. "I ain't seen no cattle!"

"There's cattle," I insisted. "She drove 'em up and then she started 'em back the way they come, wiping out her trail. Then she went into soft sand where she wouldn't leave no tracks."

"Still, they might have found her."

"Nossir, they didn't. They followed her into them hills, but they lost her trail under the hoofs of them cattle, like she figured they would. They hunted a long time, then they come back."

"Are those tracks still there?"

"Nossir. There ain't no tracks of any kind. On'y rains before that was soft and gentle, not enough to wipe out good tracks."

"Doby," Pa never called me by name an awful lot, so he was almighty serious, "Doby, why didn't you ever tell me?"

I could feel my neck gettin' red. "Pa, you was so set on this place. You takin' to it like no other an' all. An' me, I liked it, too. I was afeared if you knowed you might pull out an' leave. You might just give up an' we'd be ridin' the wagon agin, goin' nowhere much. I want to stay, Pa. I want to stay right here. I want to see our work come to somethin', an' I want a place I know is home."

"Stay on," the stranger said. "I think I can safely say it will be all right."

"But how?" Pa asked. "How can anybody?"

"I can," the stranger said, "I can say it. My name is Chantry. The dead man you buried was my brother."

Well, we just looked at him. Pa was surprised, and maybe I was, too, a little. I'd had a funny feelin' all along, only mostly I was afraid he was one of *them.*

"Even so," Pa said, "What about his daughter? An' his wife or whoever she was? Don't she have first claim?"

"That's just it," Chantry said quietly, "my brother was a widower, with neither wife nor child. He was a lot older than me. If there was a woman, then I have no idea who she was or what she was doing here."

2 Pa cut himself a piece of work when he decided to farm that place, and it taken some doing for the two of us. And from time to time I headed for them hills, Pa liking fresh meat and there being no game close by 'cept an occasional deer in the meadow.

Come daybreak, it bein' Sunday, I taken Pa's old rifle and saddled up the dapple. Saying nothing to Pa or Chantry, I just taken off.

They were low, rolling hills that broke into sharp bluffs, kind of a bench, and then the high-up mountains lyin' behind 'em. So far, I'd never been so far as the mountains, but there they lay, a-waitin' for me. They knew and I knew that one day I'd ride those trails.

Right now I had me an idea, and huntin' meat was second to that. Because that girl or woman, or whichever she was, headed right into them hills like she knew where she was going, and neither me nor them other folks found her. Least, I didn't believe they had. For certain, they never found her that first day.

If she knew where she was goin', it stood to reason she'd rode the hills before, many times maybe, and if there was any kind of a hideout, she'd know where it was.

It wasn't worryin' me much who she was. She'd either been close by when the killin' took place, or she knew somethin' about it. She surely didn't waste any time askin' questions when the shootin' started.

By now any sign she left would be washed away, 'less she was still back yonder and had cut fresh sign for somebody to follow. Any way you looked at it, she was headin' for some place and I wanted to find out where. Whatever it was, or wherever she was, she figured she'd be safe when she got there. Or that's how it looked to me.

It was cool an' pleasant. My horse had a liking for far-flung trails as well as me, and he pointed for the hills like he already known where he was going. The grass was bound to be thick up yonder, and the water cold and fresh.

I never had but just the rifle. I'd always wanted me one of them pistols, but we never had the money for it. I had me a rifle and it was a good one too— a Henry. I also carried me a bowie a man could shave with, it was that sharp.

The dapple pointed us into a fold of the hills, climbed a little bit, and we topped out on a grass knoll with the wind stirring his mane and all the world spread out before and behind.

The ranch land lay spread behind me, but I

wasn't looking back. I was sixteen year old, and somewhere in the mountains there was a girl. Now in all
my sixteen years I never stood up right close to not
more than three or four girls of her age, and ever'
single time I was skeered. They just look like they
knowed it all, and I didn't know nothin'.

That woman who rode off on that horse might be
fourteen, forty, or ninety-three for all I knew, but
in my mind's eye she was young, gold-haired, and
pretty. She was every princess I'd ever heard stories
about, and I was goin' to meet her.

For three, four years now I'd been rescuing beautiful girls from Indians, bears, and buffaloes. In my
dreams. But it never got down to where I had to talk
to 'em. I kind of fought shy of that, even in my
dreams, for I had no notion what you said to a girl.

Settin' there lookin' at the mountains I kind of
sized 'em up. Now mountains just ain't all that easy
to ride through or cross over. There has to be ways,
and if you give study to a situation you can surely
come up with one of the ways.

Looked to me like I saw a faint trail goin' up
through the grass along the slope of a certain hill,
so I taken a chance and moved out and that dapple
taken that trail and held to it.

I thought the trail seemed to peter out, but not
for the dapple. He seen or smelled it, and just kept
a-goin' and we dipped down off that slope across a
meadow so green it hurt your eyes, and then across
a rough and randy little mountain stream that boiled
along over the rocks like it was going somewhere
a-purpose, and then into the trees.

We skirted the aspens, and I seen an elk. It was a
bull elk, maybe half-grown, and fat as a tick. That
was meat for a coupla weeks plus jerked meat for

winter, and my rifle came halfway up before I stopped it.

That shot would go echoing off up that canyon and warn anybody, friend or enemy, that I was on my way. Unhappy and feeling bad, I let that elk go. But it was too soon to shoot. I had a sight of country to see before I started telling ever'body I was there.

At the edge of the aspen stand, I drew up the dapple and sat and listened. The elk kinda moved off, paying me no mind. I let him walk away, then looked up at the great swell of the mountain. It was rounded green, with a battalion of aspens marching down the slope in a solid rank til it came to a halt. Like a troupe of soldiers. From there on, it was only grass with a few dips and hollers here and there with tufts of brush showing. That trail I was following, or one kin to it, made just a little thread across that slope.

Now trails in the mountains can be game trails, but you usually don't see them from afar unless a body is above 'em. Trails can also be Indian trails, or they can be where some prospector has staked him a claim . . . or maybe even built him a cabin.

Chantry had said his brother had no wife nor daughter. Who, then, could that mysterious girl or woman be?

She might be some woman Chantry taken up with. Or just somebody he'd met or found who needed help.

The dapple walked along easy-like. We dipped down into a draw, waded a branch, and had started up the opposite slope through the aspen when all of a sudden there were two men setting their horses right slam in front of me, barring the trail.

One of them was a stocky, barrel-chested man with a broad, hard face and tiny eyes. The other man was much like him, only a mite bigger.

"Where d'you think you're going?" the smaller one asked me.

"Huntin' meat," I said, kind of careless-like. "Figgered I might scare up a elk."

"This here trail's closed, boy," the other man said. "We got us a claim back yonder. We wouldn't want to get hit by no stray bullets. So you just hunt down below or off to the other direction."

A grin broke his hard face like somebody had cracked a rock. "Why, somebody was to shoot up here we might take it wrong. We might just figure he was a-shootin' at us an' shoot back. You wouldn't like that, now would you, boy?"

He wasn't runnin' no bluff on me. I didn't cotton to him, nohow, and didn't believe he had a claim back yonder. "Nossir," I said, "I wouldn't like that. I wouldn't want nobody thinkin' I actually shot at 'im an' missed. Thing like that," I said, "can ruin a man's reputation."

Well, they just looked at me. They'd took me for some kid they could scare, not dry behind the ears, but I never was much of a one to scare.

Back yonder to home I'd heard a fussin' in the pigpen one night when Pa was gone, and I'd taken down his shotgun loaded with buckshot an' gone with a lantern to see what for. Well, I opened the door of the pigshed an' they was all backed into a corner with a full-growed cougar lookin' 'em straight in the eye. When that door opened he turned on me, ears back an' tail a-lashin'. Now nobody in his right mind corners a cougar, 'cause cornered they'll fight. But I wasn't of no mind to let that cougar make a bait of one of our pigs, so I ups with the shotgun and let him have a blast just as he leapt at me.

That cougar knocked me a-rollin', tail over tea-kettle back out the door, an' my head smacked up agin a rock and laid me out cold. But when Pa got home I had me a cougar skinned and the hide nailed up to dry out on the outside cabin wall.

"Look, kid," the bigger man said. "You're a mite sassy for a boy your size. Somebody'll take you off that horse an' give you a whuppin', if you don't watch out."

"Mebbe," I said. "But he'd be doin' it with a chunk of lead in his belly. An' if there was two of them, two chunks of lead.

"This here's a free country, wide open for all, and if you're worried about gettin' shot at, you just high-tail it back to your claim, because I reckon I could see a claim and men workin' and I'd put no bullet near 'em . . . 'less they asked for it.

"I come up this mountain for meat, an' when I go back down, I'll have it." I had that Henry right across my saddle. Both men was pistol-armed and one of them had a rifle in his boot, but it was in the boot and them handguns was in their holsters. My Henry was lookin' right at them.

"You get your meat," the stocky one said again. "But make sure you stay shy of this mountainside or you'll get all the shootin' you want and then some."

They turned their horses then and went back up the trail, and soon as they were out of sight, I reined my dapple over and whisked through the trees, myself. No tellin' when they might try to circle around an' take a shot at me.

Followin' that trail that day didn't look like good business, so I angled off through the trees, just getting myself out of harm's way. I wasn't no way eager for a shootin' over anything like that, but I didn't figure to back up, neither. So I worked my way up a slope, turned north and then west with the lay of the land and the trees, and suddenly I come out atop a mesa, riding down amongst some all-fired big ponderosas, scattered spruce and aspen. Coming down through some big old trees I come upon a cabin.

It set on a slab of solid rock with a big wide view of the whole country spread out in front. A body could see the Sleeping Ute, the great juttin' prow of Mesa Verde, and way afar off, the Abajo and La Sal mountains of Utah. Some trees growin' on the edge of the cliff kind of screened the cabin off, but a man with a good glass could of picked up ridin' men some distance away.

The builder had cut grooves in the solid rock and put in fitted squared-off timbers that were nigh two-foot through. They'd been fitted like they'd growed that way, and the roof was strongly built and solid.

I knocked on the door, expectin' no answer, and none came. So I lifted the latch and stepped in.

I got a surprise.

The place was empty. But the floor was swept clean, the hearth dusted, and everything spic an' span. There was a faint smell in the room that wasn't the smell of a closed-up place. It was a fresh, woodsy smell. And then I seen on a shelf behind me a pot with flowers in it and some sprigs of juniper.

The flowers wasn't two days old, and when I looked in the pot there was water for 'em.

There was no bedding. There were no clothes hung on the pegs along the wall, and no dishes for cookin' 'cept for a coffeepot.

Outside, there was a bench by the door, and the grass below it looked like somebody had been settin' there, time to time. That somebody could see our ranch right easy. It was miles away but the air was mountain clear, and you could see the ranch plain as day.

By now I was three miles or more from where I'd come up against the two trouble-hunters, and I'd followed no trail to get here. Yet I knew there must be a trail. Maybe more than one.

I scouted around the place, around the clearing. Now nobody ever said I couldn't read sign, and by the time I'd finished and set down on that bench I knowed a thing or two.

It was a girl or woman who come here, and she didn't come often, but when she did she set awhile. I found no tracks but hers . . . not even horse tracks.

She must have come by horse. She'd likely left it back in the brush somewheres. This was a deserted, lonely place, and it looked to me like the girl who come here liked to be alone.

Was it the selfsame girl who'd been to Chantry's place? I had me a feelin' it was. From here she could see the Chantry place clear.

Maybe, when she came here, she watched and got curious to see who was living on the Chantry place.

Maybe.

Whoever built this cabin had known what he was doin', anyway. The land sloped gently away in front of the cabin for a hundred yards, and where the grass ended against the trees there were some tall old pines that make it unlikely anybody could see the cabin from way down below, even with powerful glasses.

There was water. And beyond the pines the mountain fell clean away down through timber where no horse could go, nor a man climb up without a good struggle. Behind, there was forest that swelled up into the mountain. A trail could lead off somewhere right or left of that swell.

Suddenly I had me a idea. That woman had cleared up this place and left flowers. She liked the place and she liked it neat. I figgered to let her know somebody was about who liked what she had done. Who liked what she liked.

Under one eave of the house I found a small Indian pot. I taken it, rinsed it good, and half-filled it with water. Then I went down the slope and picked some flowers and put them in the water. This I left on the table where she'd be sure to see it.

Then I scouted for a trail to go back down and found one. It was a faint trail, but it had seen some use, time to time. First off, I looked for sign. Whatever there was seemed to be maybe a week old. I followed along, studying tracks. It was a horse that weighed no more than eight hundred pound, but with a nice, even pace. And the woman who rode that horse was small, 'cause I saw the hoof tracks when the horse was unmounted and after, and her weight didn't make hardly a single bit of difference.

Now I knew that trail led somewhere, and I had me a idea it led right to where those two men had come from, who braced me on the trail. So once I spotted the direction the trail taken, I moved into the timber and hightailed it for the Chantry place. To home.

Pa was out near the barn and he looked up when I come in. "First time you ever come home without meat, boy. What's the matter? Didn't you see nothin'?"

"Never got a good shot," I said. "Next time it'll be different."

"We got to have meat, son. I'll take a walk down

the meadow, come sundown. Sometimes there's a deer feedin' down thataway."

Chantry come out on the steps. He threw me a quick, hard look. He'd dusted off his black suit and polished his boots with a rag. He stood there on the steps, looking toward the mountains while I filled a bucket of water for the house. We all kept busy for a while, even Chantry, with his thoughts.

It was coming up to sundown now, and when Pa took his rifle and started off, Chantry just stood there watching him go. "He's a good man, your father is," he said. "A real good man."

"Yessir. We've had us some hard luck."

"This is rough country," Chantry replied. "I like what he's doing here."

"He just plain fell in love with the place. . . . All the work that somebody else had done. He couldn't just go off an' leave it be."

"I know." Chantry looked at me again. "Now, boy, tell me what you saw today."

"What I saw? I . . ." Well, I started to lie, but he was looking right straight into my eyes and smiling a little, and suddenly I didn't want to lie to him. So I told him the whole business from the start. Leaving out the flowers.

"You think she and those men came from the same outfit?"

"There ain't too many outfits around I know of. I think *maybe* it's the same outfit. She bein' a woman. . . . Maybe she's got different feelings."

"That might be the reason. And sometimes an honest person gets roped into a setup they don't rightly know how to get clear of. What about that cabin? Anything strike you odd about it?"

"Yessir. I believe it was built by the same man who

built this. The same kind of work. . . . Only that place up there is older. I think maybe he lived up there first and kept lookin' down on this flat country and decided to come down here and settle."

"Might be right. Or maybe he just wanted two homes. One up high, one down below." He looked at me again. "What's your name, boy?"

"Doban Kernohan. They call me Doby."

"Irish. . . . Well, we come of the same stock, Doby. I'm Irish, too. . . . Mostly Irish. My family left the old country a long time ago, and an ancestor of mine went to Newfoundland, then to the Gaspé Peninsula. From there to here, it's a long story."

"You got a first name, mister?"

"Owen. A name that is sometimes Irish, and sometimes Welsh, they tell me. Well, there's been a sight of changing of names, Doby, especially among the Irish.

"There was a time long ago when Irishmen were ordered by law to take an English name, and around about fourteen sixty-five, a time later, all those in four counties were to take the name of a town, a color, or a skill. Such as Sutton, Chester, Cork, or Kinsale for the town. Or the colors—any one they'd happen to choose. Or a trade, such as carpenter, smith, cook, or butler, to name just a few.

"And some of the Irish changed their names because there was a move against us. Many in my family were killed, and when my great-grandfather escaped to England he was advised never to tell his true name, but to take another . . . or he'd be hunted down. So he took the name Chantry, although how he came by it I do not know, unless he happened to see and like the name, invented it, or took it from some man he admired. In any event, the name has served us well, and we, I trust, have brought it no dishonor."

"I know little Irish history," I said.

"That's likely, Doby, but the thing to remember is that this is your country now. It's well to know about the land from which you came. There's pride in a heritage, but it's here you live. This is the land that gives you bread.

"Yet it's a good thing to know the ways of the old countries, too, and there's no shame in remembering. There's some as would have it a disgrace to be Irish. . . . You'll find places in eastern cities where they'll hire no man with an Irish look or an Irish name. A good many of those who come here are poor when they land, and nobody knows what lays behind them.

"Some are from families among the noblest on earth, and there's many another who's put a 'Mac' or an 'O' to his name to which he's not entitled. But a man is what he makes himself, no matter what the blood or barony that lays behind him."

"What was your family name, Mr. Chantry, sir?"

"We'll not be talking of that, Doby. Three hundred years gone by and every child of the family has known the name. But not one has spoken it aloud. And so we shall not. Chantry is the name we've taken, and Chantry is the name we'll keep."

"Did you come here to claim your brother's ranch? Pa says it's yours by right."

"No, lad, I came not for that. There was another thought in my mind, though t'was my brother I wished to see. The ranch will be your Pa's and after him yours—but only to keep, and not to sell. I'll make a deed that way. . . . But I'll want living quarters here when I pass by, and I think I'll claim the cabin up there the mountains are holding for me."

Something in my face drew his notice, for I was right worried, thinking of the girl. "What is it, boy? What's troubling you?" he asked.

"It's just the girl . . . the woman, sir. I believe she likes the mountain place. I believe she goes there to be alone. She left some flowers there . . ." I said.

"If she loves the place she can come when she wills, but give it up, I'll not." Owen tapped his breast pocket. "I've a deed here to all the land you've claimed and more. Even the slope of the mountain is mine, and a bit beyond it, here and there.

"Four sections your father has claimed, and those four sections he can have. There's thirty more I'll keep for myself, for I've a love for this western land, and here I may stop one day after I've done some things that need doing."

It was the most I'd heard him talk, and the most he did talk for many another day.

At daybreak my eyes opened to hear the echo of a rifle, and I came bolt upright and scared. Pa was puttin' on his pants and reaching for his gun.

But we couldn't see aught. Only that Chantry was gone and his horse was gone, too. But an hour later when he came in he had some nice cuts of venison wrapped in its own hide.

"Here's some meat," he said. "I'll not be a drone, Kernohan."

Chantry did his share of the woodcuttin' too, and he was a better than fair hand with an ax, cuttin' clean and sure and wasting no effort. Yet he stayed close to the house, spending most of his time on the porch with his glass in his hand to study the rise of the mountains.

Once I asked if I could look through it. "Yes," he said, "but handle it gentle. There's not its like in the world, I'm thinking. It was made some time ago by a man in a country far from here. He was the greatest master of his craft, and the lenses of this scope he ground himself."

It was astonishing the way the mountains leaped up at you. Far away as we were, you could almost reach out and touch the trees. I could even make out the cabin behind its trees, the bench at the door.

Was it that he was watching? I felt a pang of jealousy, then. Was he watching for her?

3 It was lonely country. When Chantry come along he brought some news. We'd heard nothing of what went on. Here and there a prospector worked in the hills, but they were shy of Indians and so kept out of sight, just comin' and goin' on the run.

South of us, in New Mexico, folks had told us there wasn't no white men at all, that those who come before us had just gone on through or left their hair in some Indian's wickiup.

Some had come, all right, as we had, but they'd not stayed and there was no record of their comings and goings. Pa found a rusted Patterson Colt once, down on a wash to the south of us. An' a couple of bones an' a few metal buttons, all that was left to show for somebody who tried to move into that country.

But there was Indians a-plenty, though a body saw mighty few of 'em. There were Utes to the north and around us, Navajos to the west and south, and Apaches east. Some friendly, some almighty mean and evil. Some just plain standoffish, wantin' to stay to themselves and not be bothered. Well, we didn't aim to bother them none.

"I never give 'em much thought," Pa said. "No more'n I would a white stranger. They're folks. They got their ways, we got ours. If we cross, we'll talk it over or fight, whichever way they want it to be."

Chantry agreed. "You can't talk about all Indians the same way, boy. Any time a man comes along and says 'Indians' or 'Mexicans' or 'Englishmen' he's bound to be wrong. Each man is a person unto himself, and you'll find good, bad, and indifferent wherever you go."

Didn't seem to me that Owen Chantry was taking any chances, though. When he put his pants on in the morning he also put on his gun belt and his gun. Most men put their hat on first. He put on that gun belt 'fore he drew on his boots.

"You figurin' on trouble?" I asked him once.

He threw me a hard look. "Boy," he said, "when a man comes at me shooting I figure he wants a fight. I surely wouldn't want him to go away disappointed.

"I don't want trouble or expect trouble, but I don't want to be found dead because I was optimistic. I'll wear the gun, use my own good judgment, be careful of what I say, and perhaps there won't be trouble."

He still didn't tell us why he'd come to start with, and it was a question you didn't ask. He was more than welcome. In them days you could ride a hundred miles in any direction and not see a soul.

Once Chantry got started he was a natural-born storyteller. Of a nighttime, when the fire burned down on the hearth and the shadows made witches on the walls. He'd been a sight of places and he'd read the stories of ancient times, the old stories of Ireland, of the sea and some folks called the Trojans who lived somewheres beyond the mountains and did a lot of fighting with the Greeks over a woman. And stories of Richard the Lion-Hearted, who was a great fighter but a poor king.

An' stories of Jean Ango, whose ships had been to America before Columbus. And of Ben Jonson, a poet, who could lift a cask of canary wine over his head and drink from the bunghole. He told of Gessar Khan, stories that happened in the black tents of nomads in haunted deserts on the flanks of a land called Tibet.

An so our world became a bigger place. He had him a way with words, did Owen Chantry, but he was a hard man, and dangerous.

We found that out on the cold, still morning when the strangers come down the hills.

I'd gone to put hay down the chutes to the mangers for the stock, an' I was in the loft with a hayfork when they come.

Pa was in the yard, puttin' a harness on the mules for the plowing.

They come ridin' up the trail, five rough men ridin' in one tight bunch, astride better horses than we could afford, and carryin' their guns.

They drew up at the gate. And one of the men outs with his rope, tosses a noose over the gatepost, and starts to pull it down.

"Hey!" Pa yelled. "What d'you think you're doin'? Leave that be!"

"We're tearin' it down so you'll have less to leave behind. When you go." The speaker was a big brawny man with a gray hat.

"We're not goin' nowhere," Pa said quietly. He dropped the harness where he stood and faced them. "We come to stay."

The two men I'd met on the trail were in the bunch, but my rifle was inside the house. Pa's was too.

We might just as well have had no weapons for the good they could do us now.

"You're goin'," the brawny man said. "You're ridin' out of here before sundown, and we'll burn this here place so nobody else will come back."

"Burn it? This fine house, built by a man with skill? You'd burn it?"

"We'll burn any house and you in it if you don't leave. We didn't invite you here."

"This here is open land," Pa said. "I'm only the first. There'll be many more along this way 'for long."

"There'll be nobody. Now I'm through talkin'. I want you out of here." He looked around. "Where's that loud-mouthed boy of yours? One of my men wants to give him a whippin'."

I'd dropped from the loft and stood just inside the barn. "I'm here, and your man ain't goin' to give me any kind of a whippin' . . . not if it's a fair fight."

"It'll be a fair fight."

The words come from the steps, and we all looked. Owen Chantry stood there in his black pants, his polished boots, a white shirt, and a black string tie.

"Who in hell are you?" The brawny man was angry some, but not too worried.

"The name is Owen Chantry," he replied quietly.

The stocky man I'd met on the trail got down from his horse and come forward. He stood there, a-waiting the outcome.

"Means nothing to me," the brawny man said.

"It will," Chantry said. "Now take your rope off that post."

"Like hell I will!" It was the man with the rope who shouted at him.

In the year of 1866, the fast draw was an unheard of thing out west of the Rockies. In Texas (so Chantry told me later), Cullen Baker and Bill Longley had been usin' it, but that was about the extent of it til that moment.

Nobody saw him move, but we all heard the gun. And we seen that man with the rope drop it like something burned him, and something had.

The rope lay on the ground and that man was shy two fingers.

I don't know whether Chantry aimed for two fingers, one finger, or his whole hand, but two fingers was what he got.

Then Owen Chantry come one foot down the steps and then the other. He stood there, his polished boots a-shinin' and that gun in his hand. First time I'd ever seen that gun out'n the scabbard.

"The name," he said, "is Owen Chantry. My brother lived on this place. He was killed. These folks are living here now, and they're going to stay.

"I, too, am going to stay, and if you have among you the men who killed my brother, your only chance to live is to hang them. You have two weeks in which to find and hang those men. . . . Two weeks."

"You're slick with that gun," the brawny man said, "but we'll be back."

Owen Chantry come down another step, and then another. A stir of wind caught the hair on his brow and ruffled it a mite and flattened the fine material of his white shirt against the muscles of his arms and shoulders.

"Why come back, Mr. Fenelon?" Chantry said pleasantly. "You're here now."

"You know my name?"

"Of course. And a good deal more about you, none of it good. You may have run away from your sins, Mr. Fenelon, but you can't escape the memory of them. . . . Others have the same memories."

Chantry walked out a step toward him, still with that gun in his hand. "You're here already, Mr. Fenelon. Would you like to choose your weapon?"

"I can wait," Fenelon said. He was staring at Chantry, hard-eyed, but wary. He didn't like nothin' he saw.

"And you?" Chantry looked at the stocky man who was settin' to whip me. "Can you wait too?"

"No, by the Lord, I can't! I come to slap some sense into that young'un, and I aim to do it!"

Chantry never moved his eyes from them. "Doby, do you want to take care of this chore right now, or would you rather wait?"

"I'll take him right now," I said, and I walked out there and he come for me, low an' hard.

My Pa come from the old country as a boy and settled in Boston, where there was a lot of Irish and some good fightin' men amongst 'em. He learned fightin' there, and when I was growing up he taught me a thing or two. Pa was no great fightin' man, but he was a good teacher. He taught me something about fighting and something about Cornish-style wrestling. There were a lot of Cousin Jacks in the mines, then as ever, and Pa was quick to see and learn. But he was a teacher, not a fighter.

Me, I started scrappin' the minute they took off my diapers. Most of us did, them days.

Here I was sixteen, with plenty of years already

spent on an ax handle, a plow, and a pick and shovel. So when he come at me, low and hard like that, I just braced myself, dropped both hands to the back of his head, and shoved down hard with them.

I was thoughtful to jerk my knee up hard at the same time.

There's something about them two motions together that's right bad for the complexion and the shape of a nose.

He staggered back, almost went down on his knees, and then come up. And when he did his nose was a bloody smear. He had grit, I'll give him that. He come for me again and I fetched him a swing and my fist clobbered him right on the smashed-up nose.

He come in, flailing away at me with both fists, and he could hit almighty hard. He slammed me first with one fist and then with the other, but I stood in there and taken 'em and clobbered him again, this time in the belly.

He stood flatfooted then, fightin' for wind, so I just sort of set myself and swung a couple from the hip. One of them missed as he pulled back, but the other taken him on his ear and his hands come up so I belted him again in the belly.

He taken a step back and my next swing turned him halfway round and he went down to his knees.

"That's enough, Doby," Chantry said. "Let him go."

So I stepped back, but watchin' him. Fact is, I was scared. I might have got my ears pinned back, tacklin' him thataway. . . . Only he made me mad, there by the road.

"Now, gentlemen," Chantry said, "I believe you understand the situation. We are not looking for trouble here. These good people only wish to live, to work the ranch, to live quietly.

"As for myself, I've told you what I expect. I know either you or someone you know killed my brother. I'll leave it to you. Hang them, or I shall hang you. . . . One by one.

"Now you may go. Quietly, if you please."

And they rode away, the stocky one lagging behind, dabbing at his nose and mouth with a sleeve. First one, then the other.

Pa looked at me in astonishment. "Doby, I didn't know you could fight like that!"

I looked back at him, kind of embarrassed. "I didn't either, Pa. He just gimme it to do."

Suppertime, watching the clouds hanging around the highup mountains, I thought of that girl and wondered what she was to them and would anything happen when they rode home.

"You don't really b'lieve they'll hang their own men, do you?" Pa asked.

"Not right away," Chantry said quietly. "Not right away."

We looked at him, but if he knew it he gave no sign, and I wondered just how much he believed what he said.

"You'd really hang 'em?" Pa asked him then.

Owen Chantry didn't reply for a minute, and when he did he spoke low. "This is new country, and there are few white men here. If there is to be civilization, if people are to live and make their homes here, there must be law.

"People often think of the law as restrictions, but it needn't be, unless it's carried to extremes. Laws can give us freedom, because they offer security from the cruel, the brutal, and the thieves of property.

"In every community—even in the wildest gangs and bands of outlaws—there is some kind of law, if only the fear of the leader. There has to be law, or there can be no growth, no security.

"Here there is no established law yet. We have no marshal, no sheriff, no judge. And until such things exist, the evil must be restrained. A man has been murdered, you have been warned to leave.

"This country needs men like you. You may not think of yourselves as such, but you are the fore-runners of a civilization. Where you are, others will come."

"And how about you, Mr. Chantry?" I asked.

He smiled, with genuine warmth. "Doby, you've asked the key question. How about me? I am a man who's good with a gun. I'll be needed until there are enough people, and when there are enough, I shall be outmoded.

"I do not recall any other time in history when men like me existed. Usually it was a baron or a chief who brought peace to an area, but in this country it is often just a man with a gun."

"I don't put no stock in guns," Pa said suddenly. "I figger there should be a better way."

"So do I," Chantry replied. "But had there been no gun today, your son would have been beaten by not just one man but several. Your fence pulled down, your house burned.

"Civilization is a recent thing, sir. With many, it's still no more than skin deep. If you live in a busy community, you must live with the knowledge that maybe two out of every ten people are only wearing the outer skin of civilization. And if there was no law, or if there was not the restraint of public opinion, they would be utterly savage. . . . Even some people you might know well.

"Many men and women now act with restraint because they know it is the right thing to do. They know that if we are to live together we must respect the rights of those around us. Our friends in the mountains do not feel that way. They've come to this remote place because they wish to be free of restraint, to be as cruel, as harsh, as brutal as they wish."

"You talk like a schoolteacher, Mr. Chantry," I said.

He glanced at me. "I wish I was a schoolteacher. It is the most honorable profession, done well." He smiled at me. "Maybe, in a sense, that's what I am."

"You say when there're enough people you won't be needed anymore," I said boldly. "How long're you givin' yourself?"

"Ten years. Maybe twenty. Surely not more than thirty. Men become civilized by degrees. By adapting, compromising."

"A man like you, with your education, I reckon you could do anything," Pa said.

Chantry's smile was grim. "No," he said. "I've had a fine education, good opportunities, but I was trained for nothing. . . . To be a gentleman, to oversee land, to direct the work of others. To do all that one must have a business, or money to employ. . . . I have nothing.

"I have read . . . and riding long distances alone has given me time to think."

"What about that woman up yonder?" Pa asked.

"She's to be considered. Most definitely, she's to be considered."

Somethin' in the way he said it made me uneasy. I liked him . . . figured he was quite some man, but he worried me, and he knew it. Suddenly I knew. That was his trouble. He *knew* the kind of man he

35

was. Whatever he done, one part of him stood off and watched.

He walked outside to the steps and lit one of them slim cigars he smoked. He stood there, away from the light, and after helping Pa with the dishes, I followed him.

"Have you seen her, Doby? I mean that girl up there? Have you seen her?"

"No. I ain't."

He was silent awhile. His cigar glowed in the dark. At last he said, "I'm going up there, Doby. Can you tell me how to get to that cabin?"

Then I was silent. There was a resentment in me. I had found that cabin my own self. What did he want to go there for? What was the woman to him?

"Don't know's I could," I said. "It ain't easy."

"Is it that you cannot . . . or will not?"

"Mr. Chantry, that there cabin is where she comes to be *alone*. She's got a right . . . once in a while. I figure maybe she needs to have her a place, and I don't want—"

"Doby," he was patient. I could sense his patience. And his irritation, too. "That cabin is mine. I plan to live there, to return there from wherever I go. I, too, need a place to be alone.

"I am not," he paused just for a moment, "going to interfere with her solitude. There are other places in the forest and mountains where she can be. But I must go there. I have business there. . . . And perhaps I wish to see her."

"You'll get her in trouble, Mr. Chantry."

"Doby," his patience was wearing thin. "You don't even know that girl . . . or woman. You don't even know who she is or what. You're making a thing out of this that it should not be."

36

"I just don't like it," I said stubbornly. "She even swept up. She dusted. She had everything to rights. She put out flowers. She loves the place like it is. . . ."

"All that may be true," Chantry said quietly. "But it's my place, and I must go there."

A thought came to me at a sudden, a chance to get the better of him. "How about your brother? Maybe he give her the right to go there. Maybe he even *give* the place to her."

It was a point, and he saw it. "Not that place, Doby," he said then. "Some other place, maybe, but not that one."

"What's so different about it?" I demanded.

"It's a whole lot different." His voice was harsh. "Don't mix into things you don't understand, boy. Just remember this: that cabin is mine, and there's a lot more to it than you know."

Well . . . maybe. All of a sudden, I didn't like him nearly so much.

Yet, a man had to be fair. What he said was straight-enough talk. This here ranch was his, and he was lettin' us have it. He couldn't be more decent than that. When he could have told us to load up an' git.

He done no such thing. Plus he'd stood by us in trouble.

But still it rankled.

Fair was fair. And it come to me that all I was sore over was because he was buttin' into my dream. I'd been dreamin' of a girl up there at that cabin, a girl who was *mine* somehow. When I'd never even seen her, didn't even know if she *was* a girl, an' not some growed-up grandma of a woman.

Maybe it was because I was kind of short on

dreams and short of girls to think on. A body needs somethin' to build a dream with. Which was why, when I come to consider it, I'd not been too anxious to meet up with that girl. . . . Because once I seen her, and her me, the dream might be gone forever.

She might figger I was no account, or she might be nothing a man could be proud of herself. Just because a woman sweeps the floor and puts flowers in a pot don't make her a princess. Nor even a girl to walk with. . . .

She might be old and fat. She might be a married lady with babies. She might be anything.

The trouble was that all my thinkin' wouldn't shake loose my dream, of her being young and gold and beautiful.

She *had* to be. She just had to be.

4 Come daylight, Owen Chantry saddled up and rode away. I watched him take a trail that went to the hills, and then I headed for the dapple.

"Doby!" Pa's tone wasn't gentle like usual. "Where d'you think you're goin'?"

"To the hills," I said. "I want to see what he's doin' up there. What he's goin' to do."

"You stay right where you are. There's work to do, boy, if we spec to make a crop and get wood laid by for winter. We ain't got no time to go gallivantin' over the mountains."

"Pa, I—"

"You leave him be. He's lettin' us have this outfit, ain't he? He stood by us, didn't he? Whose business is it what he does?"

Well, there was that girl. Only Pa wouldn't understand about her.

"Boy, don't you get no notions now. That there's a good man, but he's a hard man, too. He'll take no nonsense from nobody. If that cabin up there is all he wants, tis little enough."

Pa was right. Yet I didn't want him goin' up there. He'd change things. Maybe she wouldn't come there anymore. Then how would I ever find her?

But all the time I knew I was playin' the fool. Knowin' nothin' about her, and her not knowin' me. And who was I? Just a green country boy who knowed nothin' but horses and cattle. Scarce sixteen year old. How could any such girl be interested in me?

I thought no such thing, only I *wanted* to think it. And most of all I didn't want him to spoil it for me. So I went to work like Pa said and dug postholes and trimmed poles for the fence. But every now and then I'd stop and look to the mountains and wish I was up there under them aspen, ridin' the green trails like him.

Owen Chantry rode his black horse into the canyon below the hogback. He had ridden in a wide half circle since leaving the ranch, scouting the country with care, and taking his time.

It was all strange country, and the approach he was making gave him a better opportunity to locate the actual position of the cabin. Doby Kernohan had come upon it by accident and from another direction, and Doby's grasp of its actual situation had been less than accurate . . . or perhaps Doby hadn't wished to explain too well.

Chantry frowned thoughtfully. What was it that bothered Doby? Could it be the girl herself? But

Doby hadn't even seen her, knew nothing about her. . . .

His brother had built the cabin on the rampart. That he knew.

Chantry's left hand held the reins. His right was never far from his gun. Nothing in his years had left him trusting of men or human situations. He never lay down at night without a built-in readiness to rise suddenly to action. He never sat down to a meal with the certain feeling that he would finish.

He rode forward slowly. Kernohan had known nothing of the men who had tried to drive him out, nor of their connection with the girl. A lawless outfit, doubtless.

On his right the towering mass of the rampart reared up, walls of rock almost sheer, but broken and rough enough so a skillful man might climb, if need be. It was crowned with a forest of trees. . . . Pine or spruce, he couldn't make them out at that distance. It lay like a big long loaf, thrust out from the mass of the mountains behind it.

He studied the mountains before him. He must work a little more to the east, for the mesa seemed thus easy of access, and the faint trail he followed led that way.

A deer walked into the trail before him, unawares. It stepped slowly along, then suddenly caught a glimpse of him, ducked into the trees, and was gone. Overhead the sky was impossibly blue, with puffballs of white cloud. Toward afternoon they would bunch together, turn gray, and rain would fall. Every afternoon the rains came, never lasting for long. Sometimes the showers were intermittent.

There were no tracks in the trail he followed except the tracks of deer. This trail was possibly unknown. Yet Chantry was cautious. It never paid to underrate an enemy, to assume they knew less than they did.

Were they southern renegades, come west after the war? Some of the old Quantrill or Bloody Bill Andersen crowd?

He drew up in the dappled shadow of a clump of aspens and studied the trail ahead of him, watching the trees, the ground, the birds . . . listening.

Did they know of the cabin on the rampart? Possibly only the girl did, if she came there to be alone, as Doby believed. Doby had seen no other tracks, no other signs.

He slid his Henry from its scabbard and rode forward along the trail.

It was very still. He turned off the trail and went into the trees. When he had gone a short distance, he paused again. Through a break in the trees he could see all the land to the west, a magnificent sweep of country with the vast bulk of the Sleeping Ute topping the horizon.

He was high up, with a sheer drop of two hundred feet or so a few rods away, with trees all the way to the edge. This was the vast rampart visible from the ranch. He must be close to the cabin.

He stepped down from the black and stood listening. Far off he saw several elks come from the brush to feed. There was much ponderosa here. He walked slowly forward, crossing a wide area of bare rock swept by runoff water. He saw several old stumps from trees cut down long ago, no doubt to build the cabin he was looking for.

Suddenly he saw it, partially screened by ponderosa and spruce. He knew it had been built by his brother, who understood the use of broadax and adz,

41

of squared logs. He liked its solid look, yet he was puzzled by the chimney, which might have belonged to a still older structure. But like the cabin, it was set deep into the native stone.

Owen Chantry, in a lifetime of drifting, had looked upon many constructions with a critical eye, and this one presented some interesting aspects. At first glance it was but another log house, yet it gave evidence of care in its framing and fitting, and the choice of its site. Concealed, it nonetheless offered a magnificent view to the west, with almost equally fine views to the south and north. To the east the view was cut off by trees and beyond them the vast bulk of the La Platas, with their bare peaks, slide-rock slopes and forested flanks.

Chantry could detect no movement near the cabin. Tying his mount under the trees and out of sight, he took his rifle and crossed the sparse grass to the doorway. The latch-string was out.

Lifting it, he opened the door. Inside all was empty and still, yet freshly swept and dusted. There were two pots of flowers. The hearth was cold, the ashes long dead.

He walked back to the open door and looked westward through the trees. Screened from view, the cabin was nevertheless a perfect observation point for all that moved in the valley below—and the vast spread of land that reached out in all directions.

The air was cool with the scent of spruce. A pleasant place, certainly, and a place in which to be alone. Owen Chantry leaned against the doorpost.

The mountains showed blue with distance. Farther to the north, somewhat fainter, lay the La Sals. . . . Wild country, almost unknown country from here to there. And farther on lay a maze of canyons. Father Escalante had come through, and Rivera had explored some of it a hundred years ago. Seeking a route only, they probably had seen little of the country.

He looked around him again. For the first time in thirty years, he felt at home.

The winters would be cold, for the altitude was high. A man must lay in a good supply of food to last out such a winter, and he must have reserves within himself on which to draw.

He went inside the cabin. It was as trim indoors as out.

Thoughtfully, he examined the walls, the logs solid and fitted one to the other without crack or crevice. No chinking here, for the logs had been faced with an adz until each lay cheek to cheek against the other. . . . A wall two feet thick or more, and a handsome stone-flagged floor.

There was a ceiling and hence at the back, at least, a small loft. The hewn planks of the ceiling lay from beam to beam, fitted tightly. There seemed to be no—

He distinctly heard the sound. . . . A horse walking, a horse that came slowly forward, then paused . . . just outside.

Owen Chantry turned swiftly, rifle in hand.

5   The horse stopped, blew slightly, and a saddle creaked. Owen Chantry stepped into the doorway.

The girl was facing him, wide-eyed. For a moment they stared at each other.

"You're more beautiful than I expected," he said.

"Who are you?"

"You cannot guess? You knew my brother, I think, and he was not unlike me."

"You are Owen Chantry, then? Yes, I see his face in yours. I knew Clive. He was a good man. A silent, mysterious man, but good. Too good a man for what happened to him."

"That needs to be talked about," Chantry said quietly. "I noticed a coffeepot inside, but no coffee. Did you bring some? I notice you have a lunch."

Her eyes searched his face. He was tall, leaner than she had seen at first, but wide-shouldered. There was a deceptive stillness in his face, deceptive because she already knew much of this man.

A strange, morose man, Clive had said. Too good with a gun at too early an age. In the War Between the States, Owen had at first been a wild and reckless leader in the cavalry, a man whom the war had changed. The war, and other things.

She took the pack from the horse and walked past him into the cabin. She turned. "Will you build a fire? I think there's enough here for two, if we eat lightly."

"Eating lightly has become a way of life for me," he said wryly. "Yet there have been good times."

He went out to the edge of the woods and broke the small dry twigs off the lower trunks of several trees, the little branches that start to grow, then die. From a fallen tree he peeled bark, and then he walked back into the house.

There he knelt, crushing the dry bark in his hand, placing it on the old ashes, and then the twigs. When he had the fire going, he added the larger branches. There was a good stock of dry wood in the house, and more alongside, most of it old now, and rotting.

"You know they intend to kill you?" she asked.

"I have that impression," he said. "I met some of them but they didn't seem disposed to attempt a killing then."

"Strawn wasn't with them . . . nor Freka."

He looked around at her. "Tom Freka? And Jake Strawn?"

"Yes."

"Well, well. That, of course, changes the situation somewhat."

"You know them then?"

"We've never met, if that's what you mean. But I know them by reputation. Yes, I know them. I'd say the company you choose is not always the best."

"No? Perhaps I didn't choose them. Perhaps I was put into a situation I never wanted."

Chantry chuckled softly. "That happens to many of us. I guess the true worth of a man or woman is just how far they can rise above it." And then he added, the smile disappearing. "And I haven't risen far."

She turned and stared at him. "Do you know the whole story?"

He shrugged. "Who does? I think I know most of it. I never believed it all." He smiled wryly. "One hears so many stories. . . . Lost mines, treasures buried by outlaws. . . . The country is full of such stories, most of them pure nonsense. Most people who have gold do not bury it. Clive had no interest in gold, I think. But he had a scholar's ways, which took him to Mexico to start with. Were you close to him?"

"No, not close. He didn't confide in me." The smell of coffee reached them.

Chantry leaned back and looked out through the open door at the way the sunlight fell through the aspen leaves. "Nor me either," he said. "After he got back from Mexico, he was a silent man."

She turned around to him. "Yes, he was," she said. "And also a gentle man."

"Mac Mowatt has surmised . . . as others must have . . . that a treasure of gold was buried here, or somewhere about it. . . . But that is purely their speculation. Nothing of the kind is certain."

He smiled again, and the girl was amazed at the way his face became warm and bright. He was a man, she knew suddenly, who rarely smiled.

"Value is a matter of personal attitude," he said. "What is very valuable to one man may be utterly useless to another. Your outfit thinks it must be gems or gold."

"You don't?"

"Look," he said quietly, "none of us can know for sure. My brother was a man of letters, an explorer, a scholar, a man of inquisitive mind. To him, the most valuable thing would be a book, an ancient manuscript, a clue to some historical revelation."

"A book! Just think of that!" She was amazed. She stared at him. "Why, those men out there would go mad with disgust! They'd never believe it. They'd never accept it. All this effort for something not made of gold?"

"They have a faith," he said. "They're believers, the men of your family. They live with that one idea in mind—to find a treasure that probably doesn't exist. But you could never convince them of its non-existence."

"You truly don't believe there's gold?"

"No."

"We'll have to drink from the same cup," she said.

"Charming!" he smiled again. "It will be a privilege."

She indicated the flowers in one of the pots. "Did you leave those?"

"No. I thought you put them there." Suddenly he chuckled. "Doby . . . I'll bet it was Doby."

"He must be the young man living with his father in Clive's house below. I've seen them from here."

"That's right. He's Kernohan's son. . . . They've moved in on Clive's place. Doby's the one who whipped one of your boys."

She made a face. "That was Wiley. I never liked him. Nor Ollie Fenelon, either."

"Are they kin of yours?"

"Wiley isn't."

"I think Doby's dreaming about you," Chantry said. "He found this place, and he wasn't at all happy I was coming up here. He wants you left alone."

"I believe I like Doby."

"He's sixteen, and lonesome. I know how he's feeling because I've felt it myself. I used to dream about a golden-haired princess I could rescue from all kinds of danger."

"But you don't anymore?"

He smiled, looking across the room into her eyes. "A man never stops dreaming. I like Doby. He's a good lad. He's got a father who works hard even when the odds are against him."

She refilled the cup and handed it to him. "They'll kill you, you know, all those men. There are too many of them."

"We all must die. Sooner or later. But I don't think I'll make it easy for them. How many are there?"

"Fifteen to twenty. Some of them come and go."

"Where do you fit in?"

"Mac Mowatt is my stepfather. My mother is

dead. I am Marny Fox . . . I am told our name was
Shannach until the English made us change it."

"They're a bad lot out there, you know."

"Some of them are bad," she spoke with heat,
"and some of them are not. Some are simply loyal to
Mac Mowatt. Oh, there's bad ones among them, but
Frank is fine. He's Mac's oldest son. If it hadn't been
for Frank . . ." She hesitated. "Frank is different.
He'd prefer to be ranching somewhere. He's a good
man, a solid man, but he's loyal to his father. . . .
And he's been like a father to me."

They sat silently then, listening to the soft rustle
of the aspen leaves. Chantry emptied the cup and
handed it back and Marny refilled it from the coffeepot on the hearth. He knelt beside the fire and added
a few sticks to the coals. The day was waning and
she must leave soon. . . . There was always danger—
the danger of discovery—if she stayed long.

"It's damned foolishness," he said irritably. "Nobody even knows what's actually here.

"Two men rode north out of Mexico. One Chantry.
One Mowatt. They had something with them that
Clive considered valuable. The two men wintered
here, and then Mowatt . . . or so one story goes . . .
died here. Some say he was killed.

"And some say that started the bad feeling. Some
say it began when Mowatt was accused of deserting
Clive. It's all long ago. Over the years the story has
grown to include a vast treasure. And men have
died for believing it."

"But you don't believe it?"

He shook his head. "Marny, I just simply don't
know. But Clive was akin to us all in his interests,
which were intellectual, historical . . . what you will.

"Some of us have done well with money—damned
well in some cases—but more by accident than in-

tention. So I simply believe that Clive found something of historical interest . . . something immensely valuable to him."

"Wouldn't Mowatt have known it?"

"Possibly . . . but possibly not. Possibly he couldn't even read. There are still many who can't. Clive was a linguist."

"So?"

"He might have been bringing back proof of some fancy of his. From Mexico. And how much could two men carry? They were riding Apache country. How 'vast' could the treasure have been?"

Chantry stood up. "You'd best be getting back, and so had I."

She gathered up a few things and went to her horse. "You're going to move in here?"

"Soon."

"They'll find it, Mr. Chantry. And they'll also find you."

"Call me Owen." He smiled easily. "You won't tell them, then?"

"No . . . I owe them nothing. Perhaps I owe Mac Mowatt a little. And Frank. Frank's looked after me since I was a little girl."

"Your mother married Mac Mowatt?"

"Yes. He was much older than she, though she already had me. My real father was an army officer. Mac had known him. Mac met my mother when he came by the house to see my father, not knowing he was dead."

She swung into the saddle. "Be careful, Owen. There's no nonsense about them, and some are a bad, bad lot. In their minds there *is* a treasure, and in their minds they've already split it among them. They'll kill you as quickly as they killed Clive."

He watched her ride away and then walked back

to his own horse. He brought the black in close to the house and then he went inside. It was dark there now, shadowed and still. He took a stick and spread the coals a bit, pouring the last of the coffee on them.

Then he stood up and looked slowly around. Something was hidden here, something he must find.

He believed in no treasure. But find it he must or he would never be free and it was freedom—and this place—that he wanted.

If he could live here, sit outside on that bench with a few books, watch the sun set over Utah and . . . he would ask for no more.

Well, he might not have to be alone. For the first time, he even considered that.

6 All the day long I waited for Chantry to get back. Pa seen I was restless, and a couple of times he stopped to say something but he didn't. It was away after dark before we heard his horse come clip-clopping into the yard. He hallooed the house, then he rode on to the barn to put up his black.

Pa had left some bacon an' side meat on the table, but he only ate a mite. "I had a little something in the hills," he said.

Now I knew he taken nothin' with him, so's he must have been fed. Was it her he got his food from?

"Did you find the place?" Pa asked.

"I spent most of the afternoon up there," said Chantry quietly. "And I can see why Doby was impressed. My brother had a love for this country."

"Wonder how come he got clear up there?" Pa said. "It ain't a likely place."

"Prob'ly hunting meat," I said.

"Or searching. . . ." Chantry said.

Well, then I looked at him, and so did pa. "You mean he might have knowed somethin' was up there?" I asked him.

"My brother was a man who knew much about a lot of things. He had a gift for languages. Let him hear one . . . or so I was told . . . and inside a few days he'd be speaking it. I think when he came north he rode to a place he'd been told to find. I don't think it was accidental."

"But why?" I insisted.

He shrugged. "Sometimes a man just wants to know what happened and how." He paused. "You know, Doby, this is Ute country, with Navajos west and south of here. But even they never saw this country until about the year one thousand, when they came down from the north.

"They were migrants then, as we are now. They came, they conquered whoever was here, and they settled down. Just a few miles east of here the Utes will tell you there are ghost houses along the sides of the mesas.* No white man has seen them, but I believe the Indians.

"Who built those houses? Where did they come from? How long have they been there? Who was here first? Did the builders invent the structures they built? Or were they drawing on memories of other houses somewhere else?"

"You got a awful lot of questions," I grumbled, "but no answers."

He smiled. "That's the charm of such questions,

* *Mesa Verde National Park.*

Doby. Sometimes it's a joy just to try to find the answers. Whether you ever do, or not."

Pa taken the coffee to the table and I set there just itching to ask Chantry if he seen her, for he surely wasn't going to tell 'less I did ask. Made me mad, the way he set there eatin' and talking about nothin' that mattered. Finally, I couldn't wait no longer.

"Did you *see her?* That girl?"

"I did. I did even more."

"You mean you *talked* to her?"

"For an hour or so. Had a bite of lunch with her. Like a picnic."

Chantry looked up at me, his eyes calm. Maybe there was just a mite of laughter in 'em, too. "Her name is Marny."

"Is she kin to *them?*"

"No blood-kin. She's old Mac Mowatt's step-daughter."

Well, you should have seen Pa's head come up then. He turned straight round on Chantry. "You mean . . . you mean them were Mac Mowatt's men?"

"They were."

Pa looked like a ghost stepped on his grave. "Mac Mowatt. . . . That's a bloody outfit, Chantry. I'd no notion they were even in the country."

"Do you know them?"

"I know 'em. I knowed 'em years back, 'fore the war. They were a tough bunch then, but ever since the war they been a mean, man-killing crew. Ever since Strawn and Freka tied up with 'em."

"The big man was Ollie Fenelon. The fellow you whipped, Doby, is named Wiley."

"What's she like?" I asked him of a sudden. I wasn't payin' no mind to what he said about Mowatt and them. Or what Pa said. I was thinkin' of that girl.

"She isn't blonde . . . no golden hair and blue eyes, Doby. I'm afraid that part didn't pan out."

"She . . . *ugly?*" I asked, desperately.

"No. She's very beautiful. . . . Very. She's about five-foot four, with auburn hair and greenish eyes. Good complexion. Her name is Marny Fox, and she's Irish."

"How . . . how old is she?"

"She's an old woman, Doby. Why, she must be every bit of twenty!"

Twenty . . . four years older 'n me.

Four years! That was a lot, a whole lot. But I had to protest. "That ain't no old woman!" I said.

There was more talk. And finally I went to my room and turned in, but I lay there quite awhile. The outlines of my dream have already grown kind of mistylike. Twenty years old. . . . Lots of married women weren't that old. Still, she was pretty. Maybe even beautiful.

Right then I made up my mind. I was going to see for myself. I hadn't seen no woman in more'n a year.

Looked like I'd have to be mighty careful. From the way Pa acted, Mac Mowatt must be something fierce. And I'd heard talk of Strawn, myself. An' he was a killer sure enough.

When he was in Kansas there was talk of him. He'd killed a man around Abilene, and another on a cattle drive. You heard a lotta stories of such men in them days. Talk went up and down the trails. There wasn't no newspapers, but where a man stopped there was always somebody with a story to tell. There was talk of trails, gunfighters, Indians and the like, along with talk of wild horses like the famous white pacing stallion. That was a story ever'body heard, in sev'ral different accounts. And stories of mean steers, even the length of their horns, and of horseback rides men had taken.

Them western horses, mustang stock, were tough and wild. When they run the rough country on their own they'd travel days to water, graze far out from the holes they knew best, and range back to 'em ever' now and then for a drink.

Herds them days was big . . . hundreds of horses runnin' together, maybe sometimes thousands, and some fine stock among 'em. That surely couldn't last. Horse-hunters was always weedin' out the best breedin' stock for themselves.

Next day, I give some serious study to Owen Chantry. He was a hard man who'd rode some rough trails, and he shaped up like trouble. Still, the day he nailed that gent's hand he could have killed him . . . an' some would say he should.

I said it. He looked at me sharply. "I should have, Doby. I'm just a damn fool sometimes. I should have killed him. Because somebody will sure enough have it to do."

Then when we were alone outside, he said, "That was a nice thing you did, Doby. Leaving the flowers."

Well, I blushed. I never figured him knowing anying about it. "I found the pot, an' . . . well. I figured she was a lonely woman. . . ."

"It was a nice thing to do." He paused a moment, looking westward across the wild, broken land. "When you ride, Doby, make sure you carry a gun and keep your eyes open. That's a bad outfit up there."

"Maybe," I said.

He shot me a glance. "You think otherwise?"

"Maybe they'll get friendly, like. . . . They're *her* folks."

"They're not blood-kin."

"Ain't no matter. I ain't anxious to shoot nobody."

He just looked at me again and walked away to the end of the porch. All I could think of was riding to the mountains again. I was wishful of meeting up with that woman . . . that girl. I wanted to see for myself.

We didn't have much to say, come breakfast. Chantry talked with Pa about bringin' some good cattle into the country. On the dry side of the mountains like we were, there wasn't much water, but still, there was enough so cattle could drink, and the forage was pretty good stock feed.

Same time I was thinkin' of that girl I was also thinkin' of that golden treasure Chantry had told us Mowatt believed was there. Owen Chantry took it light, but maybe he was just tryin' to talk us out of lookin'. Somebody'd gone to a whole lot of trouble if it was just a little thing. Didn't make sense to me that a growed-up man would set that much store by anything but gold or jewels, like.

Seemed to me a mighty silly thing that a man would risk his life to save a little old book, maybe nobody but a schoolmarm would put a value on. There just had to be gold up yonder.

A thought came to me, but I put it quick away. A thought that maybe my dream was replacing the golden-haired girl with a golden treasure of coins and such. But I paid no mind to the thought. I'd not even seen that girl yet, and I'd not believe Chantry 'til I did.

Right that minute I didn't care much for him. He was a sharp, hard man, I figgered, with reasons of his own for what he done. And seen close up that black suit of his was worn on the cuffs, and the boots he polished nigh ever' night, they were far from new.

Not that Pa and me had better. But he set himself up so high.

"What was her name?" I asked him again. I recalled her name. It was a dream name that was downright pretty.

"Marny Fox. She's Irish, Doby," he said, "or part Irish. They don't much like the Irish back east. Too many of us were poor when we came. But this is a good land and we will earn a place for ourselves."

"I heard Pa speak of how hard it was. Why do folks have to be like that, Mr. Chantry?"

"It's the way of the world. Across the sea, every man has a place he fills, and it's a hard and long thing to break free from it.

"We have to earn our place, Doby, just like all the others. There's no special sun that shines on any man, regardless of religion, philosophy, or the color of his skin. There's no reason why any man should expect a special dispensation from pope or president. In this country, more than any other, you have to make your mark. You're not going to be treated like something special until you are.

"Some men become outlaws. They can't make a living honestly, so they try to do it by force and strength. But everything is against them, and they cannot win."

"A man has to have some schoolin'," I said.

"It helps. Every book is a school in itself. Each one can teach you something. But you can learn a lot by observation. The most skillful trader I ever knew, a man who started as a pack-peddler—he was Irish, too—became a mighty big man in business, and he couldn't write his own name until he was over forty.

"By the time he was fifty he could speak four languages and write as good a letter as any man. . . . He was a wealthy man before he was able to write."

"If you know so much, why ain't you done better?" I demanded, rudely. "I don't see you sportin' no pocketful of gold, an' you're out here at the bobtail end of creation with nothin' but a horse."

He looked at me and his eyes were almighty cold. "I haven't done well, Doby, because I've been following a will-o-the-wisp. Someday I'll find out what it really was." He paused a moment. "Your comment is just. I know what can be done, but I haven't done it. Perhaps there were too many rivers I wanted to cross, too many canyons I hadn't followed, too many towns with dusty streets down which I hadn't ridden.

"The trouble is with wandering that after a bit a man looks around and the horizons are still there. There are nameless canyons and rivers still unknown to man. But a mortal man is suddenly old. The dream is there still, but rheumatism and weakening strength rob him of the chance to go further.

"See me five years from now, Doby . . . or ten."

Well, I just looked at him. He wasn't payin' me no mind, just lookin' off across the country, thinkin' his own thoughts. Me, I had thoughts of my own.

Then Chantry walked out to his horse. Whenever he had thinkin' to do, he curried his horse, fussed over it. You'd think that black was a baby. Yet he cared for the packhorse just about as well.

I went inside. Pa was settin' by the fire. "Pa, you think he's speakin' the truth?"

"Who?" Pa was startled. "You mean Chantry? Course he is!"

"But maybe they had reason to kill his brother, if they done it."

"We done found the body, son. And I know 'bout Mowatt and his outfit. I heard."

"You *heard*. Ain't you always told me not to b'lieve all I heard?"

"You had trouble with 'em first, Doby."

Well, that kind of backed me up in a corner. It was true. They'd been mighty rough with me. So I just said, "That don't prove nothin'." It was a feeble answer and I knowed it.

We needed poles for fencing if we were growin' any garden, so daybreak next day I packed me a lump and taken off for the hills to cut aspens.

Aspens grow tall and slim. Just right for making a fence quick, usin' them as rails. I taken an ax and when I fetched up to the nearest grove I go down and set to.

Sixteen ain't many years, but I was strong and I'd used an ax good, and I made the blade bite deep an' fast. By noon I'd cut enough poles for the best part of a day. I looped a half hitch and a timber hitch to 'em, took a turn around the saddle horn, and dragged the poles out to where I could get at 'em when I come with the team.

I dragged the first bunch, then the second. That done, I taken my horse to the creek, and when he'd had himself a drink I picketed him on the good feed there was where I'd been cuttin' aspens, and then I set down by the stream and opened my lump.

It looked like a lump, too, the bread all squeezed up and out of shape, but it tasted almighty good.

When I finished eatin', I hunted 'round for wild raspberries but they was skimpy and small. In a good year they'd be plenty of 'em around, if a body got to them before the bears and birds. But I found a few dozen and started to turn back my horse when I seen something move out of the tail of my eye.

My rifle was on my saddle so I just squatted down at the edge of the trees, hopin' I hadn't been seen.

By that time it'd been the best part of an hour since I'd been choppin' trees. So there'd been no sound from me that a body could hear more'n a few feet off.

Lookin' up to where I'd seen that movement, I set still an' waited.

The mountain sloped up under that cloak of aspens to the very foot of that great red wall that was the rampart below the mountain cabin. The cabin itself was across the canyon and more than a mile . . . maybe two mile off. Lookin' over a canyon that way, distance can fool a man.

Mountain air, specially over here on the dry side, is almighty clear and I could see somethin' movin' at the base of the red wall. He might be atop a rock slide. That was a place I'd never had cause to go, and I didn't know for sure . . . but he was alongside the rampart.

Now my eyesight is good, and blinkin' my eyes a couple times, I set to lookin' off to one side a little and, sure enough, I saw that movement again. Something was movin' along the base of that cliff, for sure. And while I set and watched, that somebody or something—moved along the base of the wall and finally disappeared. I set there a-awaitin', but whatever it was was gone.

Now I studied on what I'd seen. It might have been a animal, but it looked otherwise to me. I believed it was a man, or a man on a horse, and whoever it was might have been lookin' for a way to the top.

If a body could find a way up that cliff, he could save himself several miles of ridin' to and from . . . an hour or more each way. And it struck me then that whoever I'd seen was him . . . Owen Chantry.

He was huntin' a quick, easy way to the top.

Well, why not? I could just as well do that my own self. Settin' back where I was. . . . Well, I pulled back fifty yards from where I'd been an' set down on a stump. Then I gave study to that red wall.

Most places it was so sheer a man would have to be a sure-enough mountain climber to scale it. But there were a couple notches on the south side of the mesa that looked right promisin'. Chantry'd been workin' north along the west face when I seen him, and when he disappeared.

I looked at the sun. Too late. I'd have to hightail it for home to get there 'fore sundown, 'cause I had to go down to the river canyon and up the other side, and I wasn't wishful of tryin' it after dark. It was a right spooky ride down and up in the daylight. Even ridin' a good mountain horse like I had.

Tomorrow . . . tomorrow I'd have to hitch up the team and come after them poles. Once up here I'd picket the team and head for the red wall.

Right then I had a worried time. What right did I have to go traipsin' off? Pa was doin' his share, and it was up to me to do mine. He needed them poles. He needed the team, and he needed me and my time. We had our work cut out for us.

Still, how long would it take? An hour, maybe two. I picked up my ax and stuff and headed for the canyon.

What if I picketed the team an' a mountain lion

come down on 'em? Or a bear? Course, most times
bears won't kill livestock, not unless they done it
before or need to eat.

We couldn't afford to lose that team, not even one
of 'em.

The bottom of the canyon was dark when I got
there, but the top was still gold with sunshine. That
trail was a hair-raiser. But it would've been more
scary if it hadn't been for part of the slopes bein'
timbered.

I fetched to the bottom. It was dark down there,
only water shinin' like silver. We splashed through
and started up to the crest. A third of the way up I
stopped to let my horse catch wind, and I turned in
the saddle and looked back.

I seen nothin', but I heard splashin' in the water,
then a hoof clicked on stone.

Me, I touched a heel to my horse an' we started
on. I didn't know what was back there, and I wanted
to make no effort to find out. This was a plumb
spooky place, and even if it was just one man, I
wanted no gunfight on that hairline trail.

When I topped out on the crest, I put a spur to
that gelding an' lit out for home. It wasn't far, but
I let my horse go. Goin' home, that was the fastest
horse. I never seen a horse had more love for home
and the stable than that one. He lit out for home
like he had fire under his tail.

The house light sure looked good! I rode into the
yard, slid off that horse, and led him into the stable.
Pa come to the door.

"Dry that horse off, boy, an' git in here. Supper's
on the table."

When I taken my riggin' off, I went to throw it
over the partition and there was Owen Chantry's

black. I hung up my saddle and spoke soft to the black, and put a hand on it.

Wiped off, yes. Curried a mite, yes. . . . But the skin was damp. I was sure the skin was damp.

When I come through the door, Chantry was settin' at the table with Pa. He looked up and smiled, and that made me sore. Who did he think he was? And how did he beat me gettin' home? Maybe it wasn't him.

Then I was wondering. Who was it out there? Who followed me up that canyon trail?

7   Owen Chantry was restless, irritable. What he wanted was something to read, but the Kernohans were not readers. There was only a copy of the *Iliad*, which had belonged to his brother. Which was odd, for Clive had always been a reader.

"Kernohan," Owen said suddenly, "weren't there any books here when you came? Clive was a man who liked reading. I would have expected him to have some books."

"Books? Oh, sure! There's a-plenty. We boxed 'em up an' stored 'em in the loft. They was takin' up space and collectin' dust, so we just put 'em up there.

"Me, I never did learn to read much, an' Doby here, he's mostly innerested in horses an' guns."

"If you don't mind," Chantry said, "I'll look those books over. Might be something to read."

"He'p yourself. I looked through a few of 'em but there ain't much there that makes much sense to me. Books by them Greeks, histories an' such. Nothin' that would he'p a man work land."

Dawn came with a cool wind off the mountains, a smell of pine and the chill of rocky peaks where some of last year's snow still lingered from the winter, awaiting the next snow.

Owen went to the woodpile and took up the ax. For a half hour he worked, cutting wood for the cooking fires. From time to time he paused, leaning on the ax and taking time to study the country. His eyes searched out every canyon, every draw, placing them exactly in his mind.

Lost Canyon lay just north, a great, timbered gash coming down from the northeast. Only barely visible from where he stood, he had ridden to it on his first scouting of the country. A creek ran along the bottom. . . . One day he would go down there.

It was one of the last areas in the States to be settled. Rivera had reached it in 1765, and Escalante had passed through in 1776. Otherwise the vast land had remained unrecorded by any white man, yet men must have ridden through, hunted and prospected here. There was always one curious rider who went a little further, or passed through going from here to there. Discoverers were only those who called attention to what they'd seen and done.

When Owen left the woodpile he climbed to the loft and rummaged through the books. The *Odes* of Horace in the original Latin did him no good at all. Clive had been the Latin scholar of the family.

There was a two-volume edition of the poems of Alfred Tennyson —a contemporary—published in 1842. Chantry had read some of Tennyson, and enjoyed him. The rest could wait. He took up the two Tennyson books and climbed down.

He opened a book when he reached the last step and looked through it, riffling the pages and glancing at a poem here and there. One page was marked by a torn piece of newspaper. It was "Ulysses."

He closed the book and put it down for later reading.

When he walked outside again, both Kernohan and Doby had gone. The team was gone, as was Doby's gelding. Owen had started back toward the house when he glimpsed three riders coming down the draw toward the house.

Chantry took his rifle from inside and placed it beside the door. Suddenly, he saw movement near a bush by the stable. His hand was poised for a draw when a voice called out, "Don't shoot, Owen!"

It was Kernohan, hoe in hand, unarmed.

"Stay right where you are or get into the barn," Chantry advised.

He was watching the riders. He knew that bay. It was a big horse, weighing twelve hundred or more and standing over sixteen hands. It was notoriously fast and had won many races around the country.

It was Strawn's horse, and nobody ever rode that horse but Strawn.

Freka would be with him. Freka was part Finlander, a troublemaker who had lived in a colony of Scandinavians in Utah until they drove him out. He was known to be a good man with a gun and had figured in several pointless killings in the past few years.

They turned into the yard and drew up when they saw Chantry standing in the door, waiting for them.

"Howdy, Chantry!" Strawn said casually. "It's been awhile."

"Fort Worth, wasn't it?" Chantry asked.

Freka was the thin, blond man in the checkered shirt. The third man was heavier, a barrel-chested fellow with a bull neck and a shaved head to whom Chantry couldn't yet put a name.

"You boys traveling?" Chantry asked them.

"Sort of prospectin' around. You ever been to the La Platas?"

"Time or two."

"Rough country, but mighty purty. How's for a drink?"

"Water or coffee? We haven't any whisky."

"Coffee sounds good." Strawn swung down from his bay, and the others followed. Slowly, they walked toward the house. Halfway there, Freka suddenly turned and looked toward the barn, pausing, then saying something in a low voice to the barrel-chested man, who was nearest him.

Owen Chantry got down four cups from the shelf and then the coffeepot. They seated themselves around the table and Chantry filled their cups.

"No sugar out here," Chantry commented. "Honey all right?"

"I favor it," Strawn said.

He was a good-looking man, his face somewhat long under a high forehead, with carefully parted and combed hair. He was a man of nearly thirty but he looked younger. He was good with a gun. He had been in a couple of cattle wars and several shoot-outs.

Jake . . . that was the third man's name. He'd used other handles from time to time, but that was his real name.

"This here's a long way from somewhere for you, Chantry," Strawn said. "I figured you for a town man."

"I like wild country. The wilder the better."

"Well, you got it," Strawn said. "There just ain't

hardly nobody around here. You could ride a hundred miles in any direction and find nobody. . . . Nobody."

"Except the Mowatt outfit," Chantry commented.

Strawn looked up, grinning. "You seen them?"

"They stopped by to visit. Didn't stay long."

Strawn stared at him, then smiled. "Well, well. You mean you backed him off? You backed off Mac Mowatt?"

Chantry refilled their cups. "You know how it is, Strawn. Mac didn't figure the odds were right. Maybe he wanted company to be present. He might have been waiting for somebody."

Strawn chuckled. "You know, I like you, Chantry. I really do. Hope I never have to kill you."

"Be a shame, wouldn't it, Strawn? Somebody sending you out on a job like that? And you so young, too."

Strawn's eyes glinted, but he chuckled again. "Good coffee, Owen. I'm glad we stopped by."

"You know, Jake, I was hoping to have this talk with you. You know me better than Mowatt does, and I don't think you ever knew me to lie."

"You?" Strawn stared. "I'd shoot the man who even suggested it."

"Mowatt is after something, Jake. He's after something that isn't even there, that never was there. I don't know all the facts, but I do know there's no treasure. There's nothing here that would be valuable to anybody but a scholar."

"What's that mean?" Freka was suddenly alert.

"It means that when my brother rode up out of Mexico he brought something he valued greatly . . . and the treasure story got started."

"So?"

"What he brought . . . and I'll admit I've never

66

seen it . . . was information. A book, a manuscript, some notes . . . perhaps a plaque of some kind. To someone trying to reconstruct history it would be valuable. But to the average person, worthless."

Freka smiled with exasperation. "You must think we're all simpleminded to believe a story like that. Why would a growed-up man risk his life for something like that?"

Jake Strawn looked thoughtful. "And if there's nothing there, we wind up empty?"

Chantry shrugged. "Did you ever hear of Mowatt giving away anything of his own? Look, Jake, you've ridden for some tough outfits, and so have I, and you know that nobody but some crazy kid, some wild youngster fights for anything but gain. . . . Not in our world. So if there's no gain in treasure, where's the payoff? You know I'm good with a gun. I know you are. I know damn well I don't want to come up against you for fun, and I don't think you want to lock horns with me for no payoff."

"And you say there's no gold?"

"I do. What I suggest is this, Jake. I suggest you and Freka talk to Mowatt. Make him lay it on the line. I know all he's doing is following a dream. Somebody told a story once, and then it was told again and again and each time it got bigger. A Chantry riding out of the desert with treasure in gold on him. With a Mowatt. How did they carry all that vast treasure?"

Strawn, Chantry could see, was half convinced. But Freka wasn't even listening. In fact, he was making a great show of ignoring the talk.

"Hot air," Freka said. "Mowatt's no fool. He knows what he's about."

"Like a hundred other foolish prospectors roaming these mountains to the east of us, hunting for gold they'll never see." Chantry emptied his cup. "Just thought I'd lay it on the line, Jake. You know me, and I know you."

"So why're you here?" Freka demanded.

"A good question, Freka. I've had a brother killed, and that's a part of it. The rest is something you'd not likely grasp.

"I've been up and down and across this country. I've gambled and fought, and I've killed men for reasons that might seem slight. I've fought in cattle wars, and town-site battles, for railroad rights of way and just about everything else. I've never had much and never expect to have, but I'd give ten years of my life to add just one little bit to the knowledge of the world.

"We Chantry's have a failing, Freka. We like to finish what we start. I know the history of my family for two hundred years the way you know the trail to Santa Fe. And we've always finished what we started, or died in the trying. It's a kind of stubbornness . . . damned foolishness, maybe.

"Look, Strawn, a million years or more ago men began to accumulate learning. Over the years more bits and pieces of knowledge have been added and all of it is building a wall to shut out ignorance.

"I think what Clive Chantry brought back from Mexico was a piece of the pattern, his brick for the wall. Maybe it was a clue to a lost civilization, maybe a treatment for some killing disease, maybe a better way to grow a crop. Maybe it's one of the books of the Mayas that didn't burn. The one thing I know is that it wasn't gold."

Freka yawned. "Jake, let's ride. This talk is puttin' me to sleep." He got up. "You talk mighty well, Chantry, but I don't buy it, not even a piece of it."

Strawn got up. "You suggestin' I lay off, Chantry?"

"No. We're mercenaries, you and me. We're paid warriors. All I'm asking is that you make sure the payoff is there. If I got up against a man of your caliber, I want to be sure I'm getting paid for it, one way or another. And I'll be paid, that I know. But what will you get out of it?

"If we lock horns, Jake, one of us is going to die. There's a better than even chance that both of us will. I've seen you in action, and you're good. Damned good. I believe you've seen me in action, too."

"I have."

"Well, make Mowatt come up with something more than hot air."

"Mowatt knows something. He doesn't go off half-cocked."

"No? How many times has he told of a Wells-Fargo treasure chest that was supposed to be loaded with gold . . . and then it turned up empty?"

"Maybe you're right, Chantry. But Freka won't buy it. He wants to kill. And he's good, Chantry, damn good."

"I hope when I find out how good he is you don't have me in a cross fire, Jake."

"Hell, I fight my own battles. You and him . . . I'd kind of like to see that."

Strawn picked up his hat and followed Jake and Freka, who had gone outside. "See you, Owen." He paused. "I'll talk to the old man."

Owen Chantry stood in the door and watched them ride away.

Kernohan slowly approached the house. "What was all that about?"

"Strawn and Freka, killers working for Mac Mowatt, and dangerous men."

69

"Taken you long enough. I figured you was old friends."

"No . . . Jake Strawn and I know each other by sight and reputation. We've even eaten in the same bunkhouse, and he rode shotgun on a stage I drove a few times. I've never seen Freka before . . . but he's mean as a rattler, and just as deadly."

"Strawn ain't?"

"Strawn's one of the best men with a gun I ever saw, and he'll take a lot of lead before he dies. He's got six bullet wounds I know of, and he's still breathing good. The men who shot at him are dead. I was just trying to convince him there was no gold, so there couldn't be a payoff. He almost bought it, but Freka didn't. Freka doesn't care."

Kernohan was silent a minute. Then he said, "Chantry, I'm goin' to pull out. Me and the boy ain't geared for such as this, and I don't aim to get him hurt."

Chantry shrugged. "Your decision, Kernohan, but you've got a nice place here. You can run cattle and do well. You've a meadow or two where you can cut hay, and there's water. You'll have to hunt awhile to find its equal."

"Mebbe. But I don't aim to get my boy shot up for nothin'. I don't take to shootin' folks. I don't want him endin' up like Strawn or them others."

"Like me?" Chantry suggested.

"Or you. I don't know much about you, Chantry, but if your stories are true you've been mixed up in a lot of shootin'."

"Yes, I have. And you're right, Kernohan. But stay . . . I'll keep them off your back. But talk Doby out of going into the hills. He's got a kind of case on that girl."

"He's never even seen her!"

"He's a boy alone, Kernohan. Don't you recall how it was? At sixteen there's always a girl you dream about. Well, she's the only one around."

"Let 'im dream. Won't do no harm."

"Not unless he ties in with that Mowatt outfit just to be close to her."

Kernohan swore. "I wondered why he taken his ridin' horse when he went after them poles!" He paused, worried. "He'll come back. I know he will."

Chantry had a sudden thought. "Kernohan, when you first got here were those books boxed up?"

"No, they was on that shelf." He pointed.

"Was there anything else?"

"No, not's I recall." Kernohan sat down at the table. "That poor man lived a bit after he was left for dead. You could see that."

"How do you mean? He'd been dead a good while, you said."

"He had. But there was writin' on the step. That's why I figured there might be treasure. He tried to write some numbers."

"Show me?"

"Sure. It's faded now. He had a stub of pencil."

They walked outside. On the riser between the first and second step was written, in a barely legible scrawl, one word:

Ten . . .

"He was layin' there, kinda bunched up. Course, coyotes or wolves might have twisted his body round some, but I figgered he started to writin' some figgers and died 'fore he got any more wrote down."

Owen Chantry straightened up, disappointed. He had hoped for a clue . . .

Clive had been a careful man. He would have

71

known that if Owen was alive he would come. And, being Clive, he would have tried to leave some message, some clue.

But there was nothing . . . simply nothing at all.

8 When I got back to where I'd cut the poles I picketed the team and taken my saddle horse. Right then I had my doubts. I had a sinkin' feeling in my belly, like. Pa would never've left a team like that, to be gone nobody knew how long.

There were varmints in the mountains, and a heavy team, picketed like that, wouldn't even have a fightin' chance against 'em. These were big horses, and most times they'd give a pretty good account of themselves if they had to fight.

But all I could think of was that girl. Owen Chantry might have been tellin' the truth, but I just had to see. I still didn't like him much, he was too durned sure of himself. I couldn't see where he was so high an' mighty.

So with one long look around, I taken off a horseback. Pa was back at the ranch, and so was Chantry. I had it all to myself. I'd scout around, then come back, hitch up, an' try to make it back with the poles before it come nighttime.

Sure 'nough, back in a notch of that rampart I found me a way up. It was a scramble, that was, but I had me a good mountain horse and we made it to the top of the mesa. A moment there, we stood to take a look.

Then I turned that horse of mine and started across

the top of the mesa to cut into the trail to the cabin.
When I come into the open, I could look off across
the country. There was a box canyon in front of me,
just off a little ways, and beyond it a fine roll of
country, timbered heavy.

Some place off thataway was prob'ly where
Mowatt was holed up. I had me a notion to ride
over there, explaining that we were neighbors an'
all, so why not be friendly? But I had another notion
that warned me that for all my words to Chantry,
I wasn't that sure. So I turned my horse toward the
cabin.

Out of the corner of my eye, I thought I seen
something move in the trees, so I turned quick in
the saddle and looked back.

Nothing.

Maybe I was a half, or three quarters of a mile
from the cabin. I walked the horse along. Here and
there I could see bare spots on the trunks and limbs,
high up off the ground where porcupines had eaten
the bark. Give 'em time an' they'll kill a good tree.

The cabin stood silent. I saw no horse, and it was
a disappointin' thing. I pulled in. I walked to the
door and lifted the latch.

Inside it was cool, dim, and still. There were fresh
flowers in the pot I'd put on the table. I looked
around some more, then turned and went outside.

An' there sat three men on horses, an' one of 'em
was that man Wiley. They just set a lookin' at me
an' grinnin'.

My rifle was on my horse and my horse was away
t'other side of them riders.

"Well, well!" Wiley was grinning. "This is the one
I was tellin' you all about."

A redheaded man I hadn't seen before had him a

rifle across his saddle. "You want I should shoot him a little?" he asked Wiley, grinning. "Maybe cut his ears back?"

"Well," Wiley scowled kinda like he was studyin' on it. "No. I reckon not. I promised myself I'd pin his ears back my own self and if you shoot 'em off, how can I?"

"Look here, boys," I said. "No use for us to have trouble, us bein' neighbors an' all. Why don't we just set down an' get acquainted? Pa an' me we're no kin to Owen Chantry. We never seen the man 'til he showed up down there."

"What's the matter, kid? You scared? Why you so friendly of a sudden?"

Wiley had got down from his saddle, taking his time. I started to move toward my horse, and the redhead aimed his rifle. "You stand quiet, kid, unless you want your guts all over the grass."

The other one, the one who'd been on the trail that first day with Wiley, he was takin' his rope off the saddle. Suddenly, I was real scared. Here I was, all alone, and them three men was beginnin' to shape up trouble. I wished I had me a handgun, and for a minute there I wondered if I could jump back into the cabin and slam the door.

There wasn't no way I could make it to the woods without bein' run down or shot. That redhead just kept a-grinnin' at me. Then Wiley started for me, an' I started to jump for the door.

But the redhead snapped a loop over my head 'fore I'd took a step, and his horse taken off at a jump, throwin' me to the ground. I'd heard about men being dragged to death, so I grabbed for the rope. But he just jerked me again, and the rope tightened. Then Wiley walked over to me, and he had him a club about four feet long.

After startin' to get up, I had my feet jerked out from under me again. And Wiley lambasted me with that club. I saw it comin' and tried to twist away. Maybe I done so a little, but he fetched me right over the shoulder with that club. An' then he started at me again. I tried to get up but that rope jerked me down, and then all I could remember was a terrible pain from them blows. Wiley swung that club. He hit me over the head, over the shoulders, and across the back.

I come to, raised myself an' run at him, butted him with my head, knockin' him sprawlin' on the grass. Then I jumped on him with both feet. They jerked me with the rope and I fell again, but when Wiley reared up over me I doubled back my knees and kicked him on the knee with both my heels.

And down he went again, roaring with pain and anger, and I rolled around and lunged at him. I think the redhead wasn't tryin' too hard, and that he didn't truly mind Wiley gettin' knocked around, 'cause he and that other feller, they sat up there laughin'.

Wiley give me another bat over the head and I went down to my knees. I could feel the blood comin' down in my eyes, and I dove at him again. He got away from me and knocked me sprawlin'. Then he came in swingin' at me, but I fetched him a kick again, and he fell.

Dazed like I was, and hurt, I could only just try to keep goin' at him. But when he got up again he just had at me. How many times he hit me, I couldn't later recall, only he beat me somethin' fierce. When I finally tried to get up, he hit me a fearful swing and I felt a terrible pain in my side an' I just fell over and laid there. All I could feel was pain, and I bit at the grass so's they wouldn't hear me groan.

Wiley walked up on me, and I heard that redhead

say, "Aw, leave him be, Wiley! You got your evens!"

"I'm gonna kill him," I heard Wiley say.

"Forget it," somebody said. "Hell, he's hurt bad. The way it is, he'll never get home. I think you busted some ribs that last time. Leave him be."

Nowhere then did I lose my thoughts. I could hear them talkin' and I didn't much care if they killed me, I hurt so bad. Finally I heard them just a-ridin' off, an' I lay there, thinkin' of night comin' on an' Pa's team with the varmints around.

Somewheres along there I kinda passed out, an' when my eyes opened again it was plumb dark, an' must've been dark for some time, because I was all over wet from dew. And cold, so cold I couldn't hardly breathe.

Diggin' my fingers into the grass, I drawed myself toward the step. I heard something movin' toward me and it was my horse. I spoke to him, "Brownie," I said. "Brownie . . ."

He come to me, snortin' a little because I smelled of blood. But he stood by me and I managed to rear up enough to catch hold of a stirrup. I drawed myself up, and a pain went through my side like a knife stuck in me, so I leaned against the horse, and whispered to him.

My head throbbed an' I was sore. I wasn't goin' to get into that saddle. There wasn't no way could I make it. Best thing to do was get inside that house and get a fire a-goin'.

Somehow I got the reins up and looped them over the pommel. Then I got my rifle from the scabbard and I taken my saddlebags with my lump in 'em. Then I kinda leaned on the rifle and slapped the gelding on the hip and said, "Go home, Brownie! Go home!"

Brownie walked off a ways and stopped. That horse

didn't want to leave. Then I must've passed out again, 'cause I was cold and shivering when next I opened my eyes. Somehow I crawled inside. Dragged my rifle with me, and got the door shut.

There was fuel there, and a fire fresh-laid. I managed to get it alight, fed it some sticks, and passed out again.

During the night I half woke up, sick and moaning with pain. The fire was down. I got more sticks on it and saw the coffeepot.

There was a mite of coffee left but not near as much as I wanted. I nudged it into the coals. Then I set, shiverin', feelin' that terrible throbbing in my skull and the pain in my side and a rawness and soreness all over.

At no time was I more'n half conscious, but when I come to again—woke up by a pain, I guess—there was a smell of coffee in the room. I had me a old cup in my saddlebags with my lump, and I got it out and spilled coffee into the cup. I got myself a swaller or two and spilled some over my lips. They were all swole up, but the coffee tasted good. I passed out again, all torn up with pain and sick and wishin' I'd listened to Chantry and never come up here at all, nor trusted them people.

She found me. That girl. I was almighty sick and she come across the mesa to the cabin and found me there. It was full daylight and I was conscious but I couldn't move anyway. I was just layin' there, all sick and sore and knowin' I was goin' to die.

Laying there half-dead I'd heard a horse a-comin'. At first I figured it might be Brownie, or them men comin' back, but it wasn't no wanderin' horse. That horse come right up to the cabin and I heard a saddle creak.

Somebody said somethin'—I guess it was when she

seen blood on the stoop. And then the door opened and I heard a gasp. It was like in a dream, or when you're only half-awake or somethin'. I felt a hand touch my shoulder and turn me on my back, and it hurt somethin' awful and I cried out.

Next thing I knowed I heard breakin' wood and smelled the smoke and heard a fire going. I could hear the pine wood crackle and smell it, too. I knowed I was in bad shape, but there was just nothin' I could say or do.

She taken some cloth and wiped off my face, cleanin' up the cuts and dabbin' here and there at me. Then she began to work over me with her fingers, testin' for sore spots an' breaks. When she touched my ribs I gasped right out.

She went out for water and brought in some more wood. And once when my eyes were open I glimpsed her. She sure was pretty, on'y she was no blonde. She had no golden curls, but her hair was kinda dark red, like, with a little bit of gold in it, and prettier'n any gold-haired girl I ever seen.

"Pa," I whispered. "I lef' Pa's horses. . . . I was cuttin' poles. I lef' 'em."

"Don't worry 'bout it," she told me. "They'll be all right."

"Pa sets some store by that team. I got to—"

"You just lay still. We'll get word to your pa. I'll go get the team later."

She made up soup and got some of it in me and I felt her fussin' with a finger that was hurtin'. Somewhere along there I faded out again, and when next I knowed anything I heard him talkin'. Chantry.

"His horse came home," Chantry was saying, "and I made sure his father stayed to watch the place. Just like them men to burn it down if they get a chance."

"Did you come straight here?"

"Backtracked Doby to the team. They're all right. I watered them and changed the picket pins and then headed up here. He'd found a way up the face through a notch, so I followed him. I knew he'd come here."

Chantry come nearer and stood over me. I felt like I was a hundred miles off, driftin' in some dream world. The voices came through, but faintly. "He's taken quite a beating," I heard him say.

"I think some ribs are broken, and he has a broken finger."

Chantry touched my hand "See? A rope burn. They roped him and he tried to grip the rope. That means there were at least two of them, probably more. This boy's a fighter."

He was checkin' my body. I felt his fingers at my ribs, an' winced from their pressure. After awhile I heard him say, "We'll splint that finger. And we'll tear up his pants and bind them tight around him to hold those ribs in place. I've known ribs to knit with no trouble.

"The rest is mostly cuts and bruises. Whether he's hurt worse, only time will tell. He took some nasty raps on the skull."

"How can we move him?"

"A travois. The same way the Plains Indians carried their goods and their wounded. I'll cut a couple of poles and we'll rig up a travois."

They talked some more, and then he was gone. When I next figured out where I was, we was alone in the cabin, me and her. I opened my eyes. Every part of me was sore, and my head throbbed some-thin' awful.

When she seen I was awake she come over and

79

spooned more soup into me. It tasted good. "Thanks," I mumbled.

"How many of them were there?"

"Three. One of them put a rope on me, but I put Wiley down. I put him down two, three times. We fought all over the place. That redhead—"

"Thrasher Baynes."

"He left me just loose enough to fight. I figgered maybe he didn't mind all that much if Wiley got hurt."

"He wouldn't. Thrasher doesn't care much about anybody. But he appreciates nerve. If you showed grit, he'd like it."

"I marked him. I marked Wiley."

"Good for you. Now rest."

It was a mighty long trip down that mountain. The team followed behind, draggin' the poles I cut. There was times when I knew what was happenin' and times when I just passed out. And times when the joltin' down the trail hurt something fierce. But they taken me home, Chantry an' her.

Pa was there with his gun. He was standin' by the gate watchin' us come in, and he was nigh to tears when he seen me. Pa's not a cryin' man.

"He looks worse than he is," Chantry told Pa. "That's a tough son you got there, Kernohan."

"He's a good boy," Pa said. "He's always been a good boy, an a he'p to me. I figgered to take up land so's he could make a better start than me. But I don't know. All this, I might just—"

"Don't. You stay on. This is a good place." Chantry suddenly changed his tone. "This is land bought legally from the Indians. When the time is right, I'll transfer title to it."

Long after they had me inside and in bed, I heard the murmur of her voice out there with them. She wasn't blonde with golden curls and all, but she was pretty, she was almighty beautiful. And twenty wasn't so old. Why next year I'd be seventeen, and I was a man growed. . . . And she even said I had nerve.

Later, some time later, I heard Pa say, "If there's nothin' there, an' you know it, why don't you just tell 'em?"

"I tried to. They believe too hard, Kernohan. Men will give up anything rather than what they want to believe. And hate you for telling them there's nothing to believe. And even if you prove it to them, they'll continue to believe, and hate you for proving them foolish. Sometimes they give up, but they'll like you no more.

"I've seen men come to a ground where treasure was said to be buried, and with holes all over the hills, they'll dig another one, and then another.

"One thing I know, my brother was here for some time. If there was anything of value here, he would have found it. And being a methodical man, I believe he would leave some clue."

Chantry paused. "Moreover, knowing him, he would probably leave such a clue as only I would be apt to discover."

"What kinda clue could that be?"

Chantry shrugged. "I will have to remember what passed between us, and which of my tastes he knew best. Clive was a fine man, a much better man than I in every moral way. But he had a complicated mind, and so have I, and any clue he left would be useful to no one else."

"Well," said Pa, "for the life of me I can't figger out what kinda clue, or how you'd ever guess it."

"I've got to go back," Marny said.

Chantry turned toward her. "Don't. Stay here."

"No, I've got to go back. At least one more time. I have things there. . . . Well, I want them. I'll need them."

"Will they know you've been to the cabin?"

"No. I don't think so. But they'll go there now. Mac Mowatt will be certain he can find what there is. They'll tear the place apart."

"Maybe not," Owen Chantry said. "Maybe I'll be there."

"Alone? Against them all?"

"I won't be inside. I'll keep some freedom of action." I heard Chantry walk across the room. "Yes, I think I must do that. I must be there when they come. I want to keep that cabin."

"It's lonely," Pa said. "It's a mighty lonely place. Of a wintertime a man could be snowed in. That house must be nine thousand feet up."

"I've been up high before."

I never seen her go. She just taken off and was gone when I waked up, with only the faint smell of her perfume left in the air. But I was scared for her . . . *scared.* I had a bad feeling about her going back.

I tried to sit up and got such a stab of pain in my side that I laid down quick, gasping for breath.

She was gone. There was nothin' I could do.

If I just had my old rifle and was up in them rocks . . . well, maybe I couldn't do nothin', but could surely try.

Suddenly Chantry stood over me. "You all right, Doby? I heard you cry out."

"Didn't mean to. Yeah, I'm all right. But I wish you'd bring her back. That's a bad outfit. I wish you'd fetch her, Owen Chantry."

"I'll be at the cabin. She knows that."

"If she ever gets there. Mr. Chantry, I'm scared. I'm plumb scared for her. She don't think they knew she knowed about that cabin, but they prob'ly seen the flowers there."

Chantry looked grim, and he had a face for it. He was a right handsome man, but there was a coldness in him sometimes that would frighten a man.

"I'll just go see, Doby. I'll ride up there. Right now . . . today."

He wasted no time. He got on the big black and taken his packhorse and headed for the hills. And seein' him ride out, I wondered what would happen when him and the Mowatts come together.

Maybe he was only one man and they was many, but she sure wouldn't be no one-sided fight. Not with him being the other side, no matter how many they had.

There was somethin' about that man that made you believe. Even me, who up til then hadn't wanted to believe much of anything 'bout Owen Chantry.

Somehow, busted ribs and all, I had to be there. I had to be up on that mountain when the shootin' started.

9   Owen Chantry was a man without illusions. Nothing in his experience had given him the idea that he was protected by any special dispensation from Providence. He had seen good men die when the evil lived on, and he was aware that he was as vulnerable as any other man.

Yet a man doesn't command a cavalry outfit, scout

for the army against the Indians, drive a stage and ride shotgun without acquiring a feeling for the possibilities.

Chantry's life was due to his own skill and to a certain amount of sheer coincidence. For if he was a foot past the spot where bullets struck, it was only circumstance and the fact that he was moving faster or slower than the men the bullets found.

Owen Chantry had asked no favors of destiny. He put himself in the hands of his own skills, a good horse, and a good gun.

Crossing the canyon at a place where another canyon joined it from the east, he climbed a rough but not too difficult trail. It was timber country. There were many dams among the aspens, which were favored by beavers and elks.

He took his time. At this altitude a man did not hurry, not even with a mountain-bred horse. Mac Mowatt was a tough old renegade who knew every trick in the book and could invent more on the spur of the moment. Nor were his followers to be taken lightly, for they were all bred on the frontier. To a man.

Chantry paused near a beaver pond, letting the horses drink a little while he studied the mountainside.

Always he was careful to stop against a background where his body merged easily into the colors. From a few yards away, he was almost invisible to the casual eye.

He studied the mountainside with no sweeping glances, but with a yard by yard survey, leaving no tree, no rock, and no shadow unobserved. Occasionally, he took a quick glance back over what he had just examined.

A squirrel leaped to a branch nearby and eyed him curiously. A few yards off, another descended a tree trunk headfirst, pausing to look around. Owen Chantry spoke to his horse and turned into the aspen, weaving through the slim and graceful white trunks, around deadfalls and occasional boulders, fallen from the mountain.

The hogback, a ten-thousand-foot ridge—timbered on top, the sides rugged and almost sheer—thrust out from the mountain just below a peak called the Helmet. Before him were the towering cliffs of the Rampart Hills. He avoided the route that he had first taken around to the back of the hills, but turned toward the trail Doby Kernohan had discovered.

His problem was simple enough. He was to get Marny Fox out of there and, if there was time, to get whatever it was they were all looking for. Not for a minute did he believe it was gold.

Tracks of deer and elk were everywhere, and twice he saw the tracks of a grizzly, distinguished from other bears by the long claws on the forepaws. He noticed a log the bear had ripped open to get at the termites.

Once he paused near a small stream to watch a dipper bob up and down on a rock. He saw a school of trout lurking in a shady place where a branch hung low on the water. No amount of seeing ever made nature old to him, and he was conscious of every movement and every sound.

It was very still. Sitting his horse among the trees Chantry could look up above the towering red cliffs at the clear blue sky, tumbled with banks of fleecy white clouds.

Somewhere he was conscious of movement. It was no sound he heard, but simply some feeling, some sense that alerted his nerves. He put a hand to the stock of his rifle, then stayed it. He could feel the weight of his pistol and sat quietly, listening.

No sound. . . . Touching a heel to the ribs of the black, he started forward, holding to the thickest stand of trees. He sat up straight, weaving among them, emerging suddenly into a small clearing. He crossed it at a fast walk.

He was now almost directly under the cliffs. Again he paused to listen, studying the narrow opening before him. Chantry swore softly under his breath. He had no love for such places. A man up in those rocks with a rifle. . . .

He rode forward swiftly, trotted his horse to the gap, and then started up. It was a steep climb, but the sooner up the better.

Topping out at the head of the draw he rode swiftly into the trees, then drew up and dismounting, tied his horse with a slipknot as usual and walked back through the trees. Taking a careful look around, he then moved to the head of the draw and crouched down among the brush and rocks, waiting.

Several minutes passed with neither sound nor movement. Confident that he had not been followed, he moved back into the trees.

Mowatt now knew the cabin was there. If he hadn't already torn the place up looking for what he hoped to find, he almost surely would. Waiting where he was, Chantry sat down and considered again what he knew of his brother.

Had Clive hidden it there? Or had he hidden it elsewhere? Clive had always been a cautious man, who left no page unturned, no aspect unregarded.

What could the clue be? And where?

He and Clive had been much apart, yet there had

always been understanding between them, and a taste for the same things. Clive had been more bookish and, if anything, even more of a loner than Owen.

His love for wild country had been deep and abiding. His understanding of it, also. There had been a kind of poetry in the man. He was a man who could live richly and well without money, as long as he had wild country and books.

He must try and place himself in Clive's position.

Clive had not intended to leave here, but to stay. He would have considered all aspects of what that meant—including being killed or dying. He would have planned to leave some word behind for Owen.

Mounting his horse again, Owen wove a careful way through the aspens. It was no simple thing, for the trunks stood close together, and there were many deadfalls.

The wood of the aspens broke easily and was subject to attacks from insects as well. Consequently they fell, making travel difficult. Many wild flowers that grew under the aspens sprang up quickly as a rule. It was an unexpected route he was taking, so his tracks might not likely be found.

When he drew near the cabin he dismounted and led the black into a shadowed place where the growth was thick. He tied it, leaving line enough so the gelding could crop the grass and flowers close by.

Moving out of the aspens into a thick stand of spruces, he worked his way closer to the cabin, then squatted down and watched it for several minutes. His eyes searched the grass and could discern no evidence of passage since dewfall. No smoke came from the chimney.

He must spend as little time as possible inside the

cabin. He pictured it in his mind and went over each wall with a careful mental scrutiny. Then he devoted some time to the chimney, made of slabs of country rock, carefully fitted. He was mentally searching the cabin to cut down the time he must spend inside. But he found no likely hiding place there for treasure.

The walls were solid—carefully hewn logs fitted with care and precision. The windows, of which there were three, were actually little more than enlarged portholes, a little taller than wide, each closed by solid shutters that were tightly fitted and double-latched in the middle. They could thus be kept small, and the shutters could be set ajar to direct a breeze into any corner of the room. Yet the windows had been cut through solid logs and offered no hiding places.

The hearth was possible. But knowing Clive, Owen dismissed it at once. The hearth was too apparent, and whatever Clive might do he would never be so obvious.

No . . . it would have to be a clue that would be a clue to Owen alone. Some interest, some knowledge they shared; something Clive would know Owen would understand and that would be understood by no one else.

Rifle in hand, he left his cover and walked across to the cabin. Lifting the latch, he thrust open the door. It creaked on its hinges and swung slowly inward. The room was empty.

Standing just inside the door, Owen Chantry listened, but heard nothing. A quick glance around the house showed no evidence of anyone's presence there since his last visit.

Turning slowly around, he looked for anything he might have missed in his mental survey of the cabin.

He found nothing. Unless one tore the cabin down, the house could reveal no hiding place. The planks of the floor were tightly fitted. The flagstones of the hearth offered no hidden crevice.

Where then?

For a moment Owen stood looking out the doorway, across the grass and into the distance. Then he looked through each window. He saw the timber from which he had come, the forest behind the house, and a rugged mass of rock, trees and brush.

If he knew what he was looking for, it might be helpful, he thought wryly. If he knew the size, the kind of thing. But he had no clue.

The number ten written on a step. . . . A clue? Or something just written there in passing . . .

Ten what? Ten feet? Yards? Miles? And in which direction?

Chantry studied the earth outside, made a circle of the cabin, ten feet out from its sides. . . . Nothing.

He tried to find ten trees, ten rocks, anything in some shape or design or line that might provide the answer to that mysterious ten. He found nothing.

He looked up. There was a loft, or at least an air space between the ceiling and the peaked roof. He saw no sign of an opening, yet it could be there.

Suddenly he heard a horse approaching. Turning quickly, he glanced through the window. One man, on a gray horse with black mane and tail—a long, rangy horse built for speed and staying power.

The man looked to be around forty-five . . . perhaps a year or two younger. He drew up outside.

"Chantry?"

Owen Chantry stepped to the door, and they studied each other.

The stranger was a quiet-seeming man with strong

features and blue gray eyes. On this morning, he was unshaven. His gray handlebar mustache was shapely, however, and he was dressed neatly if roughly.

"I am Frank Mowatt."

"I've heard good things of you," Chantry said quietly. "Marny Fox said them."

"She is with you?"

"With the Kernohans, I hope." The question had surprised him. He had supposed she was with them, as she was not here.

"No, I just come from them . . . near them, at least. She isn't there."

"And she's not with you? Your outfit, I mean?"

"No."

"That doesn't make sense. If she's not at one of those places, then where can she be?"

Frank Mowatt's worry was apparent. "Look, Chantry, we may shape up to be on opposite sides in whatever happens next but I'm for that girl. She's a fine girl, and her mother was a fine woman. I want you to know."

"We won't argue the point, Frank. There's no reason she should be caught in the middle. I'm with you all the way, as far as Marny is concerned. Now all we've got to do is find her."

Frank Mowatt shoved his hat back on his head. "She come to me last night. Said she was pullin' out. I told her it was the smartest thing she could do. Said she was tellin' nobody else. Well, I got to worryin' about it and went to her shack.

"She was gone, all right, and her stuff with her. All that she aimed to take. I started out to trail her, but lost her sign back yonder on Turkey Creek. I cast about but couldn't find no tracks, so I decided to ride on over to the old Chantry place. She wasn't there, so I hunted for this place."

Owen Chantry frowned. He looked up suddenly, "Frank, are any of your outfit missing? Tom Freka, for instance?"

"Why him?"

"He's had trouble before. A dance-hall girl was killed down Fort Griffin way. The murder was never pinned on Freka, but a good many figured he was guilty."

"I didn't see him around, but that don't cut no ice. I don't see much of either him or Strawn at any time."

Chantry waited, thinking. There was a kinship between himself and this man, this tired, lonely man tied by a blood relationship to men who seemed not to be his kind.

Where would Marny go? In all this vast wilderness, where *could* she go? Obviously, she'd try to ride to the Kernohans. They were close and she knew them, and she also knew Owen Chantry.

Knew him? Well, possibly not. At least, they had talked. They had seemed to share a certain unspoken understanding, a certain warmth. Was it only their loneliness? Or was it something more?

One thing was certain: She must be found; she must be protected.

It was a curse of the Chantrys—and perhaps of all the Irish—that they belabored themselves with sorrow and old sadnesses, old griefs.

"Go back, Frank. If she returns, she'll need you."

"I could do nothing for her. Among us it is my father who decides."

"Even over the will of Strawn?"

Frank Mowatt stared at him. "Can you doubt it? If you can, you know nothing of Mac Mowatt. Wherever he is, he is in charge."

"I came out today to find her, Frank. I may have to come your way."

"They'll kill you, as they did your brother."

"If they kill me, Frank, I promise you this, you'll have some dogs to bury at my feet. Don't judge me by what happened to Clive. He was more trusting than me . . . and not nearly so good with a gun."

"Strawn said you were good. Very, very good."

"I'm not proud of it. I do what has to be done when the moment comes. And no more than has to be done. I'll find her, Frank."

"Are you in love with her?"

"I would like to find out. And so, perhaps, would she. It is not an easy thing to know."

Frank nodded. "Yes. I do know. . . . There is compassion, sympathy, companionship. All are important," said Chantry.

"They are," said Frank.

"Frank?"

He turned to look at Chantry.

"Can't you talk some reason into them? I don't think there's any treasure here. Nothing they could possibly want. They don't even understand anything but gold or treasure or money of some kind."

"You don't think there's treasure buried here?"

"Why the hell would Clive bury it? If there was treasure—and if he was a man who valued such things—he wouldn't bury it. He'd take it to where he could spend it."

"But if he didn't have time to get away?"

"Think, man. He had time to build this place, and believe me, for a man working alone that took time. You've worked with tools. He had to have time; he had to have patience."

"What could it be besides gold?"

"What I've said. We Chantrys have a love of history, of knowledge. What I think was left here is some odd fragment to an unfinished piece of history, something in the way of a clue."

"You don't know that."

"No . . . I don't. But I do know my family. And although we've sometimes had money we've never placed much store on it."

Frank chuckled, suddenly. "Be a joke on Pa . . . and them." He smiled a rare smile, then shook his head. "They'd never believe it."

"Do you?"

Frank hesitated. "I don't know . . . maybe." He looked embarrassed. "I never had no education to speak of. Most of two years of schooling and some newspaper reading here and there. I read a whole book. Never did own one though."

Owen Chantry felt the man's half-understood longing for something beyond what he knew.

"There's no end to what a man can learn if he's of a curious mind," Chantry said quietly. "And we Chantrys have been blessed, or cursed, with such minds."

"You better light out," Frank said, suddenly. "They don't aim to wait around. You're here, and they figure you know something. They'll be out to either kill you or make you talk."

"I'll be around," Owen replied coolly, "but I like you, Frank. I think you're a good man, too good for that lot. Do me a favor . . . don't stay with them."

Frank looked around at Chantry, as he turned his horse. "They're my family," he said. "I'll ride with them."

And he rode off, walking his horse, then lifting it to a trot. Owen Chantry watched him go, then turned back to the cabin.

Once more he looked quickly and carefully around.

Nothing . . . not a clue. If there was anything left here it wouldn't matter. If he couldn't find it with his knowledge of Clive's thinking, they would not either.

He went outside and crossed to the trees where his horse was waiting. It was time to go.

First, before anything else, he must find Marny.

Fear mounted inside him, fear and helplessness. Where, in all this empty land, would he find her?

10　　Owen Chantry rode his black horse north. Too much time would be lost in returning to the Kernohans to tell them of his intentions. It was better that he didn't. It would be just like Doby to try to follow, and Owen wanted no interference. Big country it was, a vast and empty country.

He rode due east as the country would allow until he struck a north-south trail, the one he had first followed to the cabin on the rampart. Now he turned north. Frank's tracks were in the trail dust, and Owen rode swiftly, noting by the tracks that Frank had also traveled fast.

Chantry was riding into enemy country, so he carried his rifle in his hand, ready for action—or, if need be, to leave the horse and take to the timber.

The tracks of another horse came off the mesa north of the box canyon and cut into the trail. This rider, whomever he was, had been just ahead of Frank.

The air was cool and very clear. During a pause to study the trail ahead, Chantry took a deep, long breath of the fresh mountain air. Judging by the growth about him, he must be almost ten thousand feet up.

High overhead, an eagle circled against the blue. In the distance thunder rumbled . . . the usual afternoon rain shower would be coming. Lightning hurled its flashing lance against the darker clouds. His black moved on, of its own volition, and Chantry let the gelding go, ears pricked, aware of its rider's alertness.

He shifted the rifle in his hands. The trail he now rode was fresh.

The trail forked suddenly, and Chantry drew up. The trail dipped down and crossed a shallow river. The water was clear and cold, running swiftly over and among the rocks. He crossed over and went up the far bank. He rode up the trail, studying the tracks.

Five horses . . . and one that held to the outside of the trail, the prints were clearly visible in the grass and wild flowers. He had seen the tracks of Marny's horse before, and he believed he was looking at them again.

He moved swiftly, deeply worried now. He was in the bottom of the canyon, which at this point was close to a half mile wide. He forded another creek coming down from the high country and went up the canyon wall through a gap where the wall had fallen back from its usual line and was somewhat lower.

Suddenly the tracks changed. For an hour, Chantry examined them. All the horses had started to run. How long ago? An hour? Two hours? Longer, surely, than that. Apparently the rider of the first horse, the outside one, which he believed had been Marny, had sighted her pursuers and broken into a run. At a dead run, she had ridden a twisted, winding trail down through the trees toward a large clearing, and here and there her horse had actually leaped over deadfalls. Then, suddenly, at the crossing of another trail that skirted the large clearing, the tracks of her horse just vanished!

The pursuers had apparently reined in, too, studying the ground. The trail that Marny had come to led east and west, but which way had she taken?

Where had she gone?

Her pursuers had turned to the west, riding hard. Owen Chantry took his time considering, for he did not wish to make the mistake they had made. Marny's life might depend upon it.

They had made a mistake, for their own returning tracks were here and there imprinted upon their outgoing tracks.

Still Chantry had not moved. Slowly he began to cast about. She was an uncommonly shrewd girl, who knew the wild country, and she had here decided, he thought, having gained a little time, to lose them.

He had to guess. . . . He had to surmise what he could not know.

He turned west, climbed over the end of a comb-like ridge that pointed north from the mountain ahead of him—a peak that looked to be thirteen thousand feet high or more. He crossed another meadow at a fast trot, watching the grass for any sign of passage, and skirted another lake.

Suddenly he was on a trail, a dim trail, long unused. It led north past some beaver ponds and some standing but stark dead trees, and into the deepening shadows of the forest.

Here it was damp and cool. He could smell the forest itself, the pine smell, the spruce smell, the smell of crushed greenery and the faint perfume of flowers.

He drew up sharply. A sound . . . something moving. His gelding snorted and tried to turn, and then he saw it.

A huge grizzly on all fours, almost as tall as his horse and weighing half again as much. The bear was in the trail before them and showed no inclination to move.

Owen spoke softly, calmly, to his horse and kept the rifle in his right hand. The horse stirred its hoofs, eager to be off.

The bear stood up, staring at them through the vague half-light. "It's all right, boy," Chantry said calmly, speaking both to his horse and the bear. Then he added, and he spoke only to the bear, and a littler louder. "We're not hunting trouble. You go your way and we'll go ours."

A bear does not charge when standing on two feet, and the big grizzly was probably more curious than anything else. A bear prefers ants, grubs, berries, nuts, and roots, and only a few become consistent meat eaters.

The black gelding reared, snorting. The bear looked a moment longer as the gelding's hoofs came down to the trail. Owen Chantry steadied the horse, talking quietly, but keeping his rifle ready.

At that distance, if the bear should elect to charge, they were in plenty of trouble. A bear can move fast for a short distance, and this one looked to be a monster, although in the dim light he probably looked larger than he was. The gelding was fast and could turn on a dime. It might be best to chance a shot and run, but the path beyond the bear was where Chantry wanted to go.

Finally, after what seemed a very long inspection

and when Chantry could hear the bear sniffing to study their scent, the big bear turned calmly and walked into the woods.

Chantry waited, holding the horse steady until he heard the sounds of movement die away. Then he rode on down the trail. "No use to get spooked," he said, speaking aloud to the horse. "He was just curious."

Now it was too dark to see tracks, and Chantry trusted to the gelding. The horse would hold to the trail, and by its ears and actions Chantry would know if anything was close by that needed his attention.

He rode on, walking his horse along the uncertain trail. Night when it came was cold. A small wind crept down from the icy peaks above. Timberline was only a thousand feet above him, more or less, and a vestige of last light clung there.

He made his camp by moonlight, gathering his wood from the broken bones of fallen trees. He could hear running water from some small stream of melting snow, and where the shelter was best he built a small fire and made coffee. He chewed on a strip of jerky and looked out across the vast blackness toward the stars in that grayer blackness overhead.

How many lonely campfires? How much incense offered the gods of desolation from his nightly resting places? And how many more to come?

He smiled wryly and got out his frying pan.

He pushed a couple of pine cones into the flames to make the fire flare up. He was in a reckless mood, irritated at not finding Marny Fox and afraid he might never find her.

He shaved bacon into the pan and put it up on a couple of rocks and watched it bubble and spit.

"Hello, the fire!" A voice called from out of the night and the cold.

"Come in, if you're of a mind to. And come any way as suits you."

A horse walked up to the fire, a gray horse bearing a gray man in the saddle. A gray old man in buckskins, with young gray eyes a-twinkle in an old gray face.

"Seen your fire," the old man said. "Figured you was wishful of company."

"I was, but I wasn't expecting you. I was expecting trouble."

"Seen a mite of it myself, time to time. I don't know's I care for no trouble, but the smell of bacon an' coffee is durned near worth whatever comes."

"Get down then, and sit up to the fire." Chantry watched the old man with a careful eye. He carried a Sharps .50 and a bowie knife, at least. If he had a handgun, it was not in sight.

"These are lonely hills," said Chantry.

"They was," the old man said, fussing with his saddle. "They was almighty empty for many a year. A man could live out his time 'thout bother from other folks. I seen more folks t'day then I seen all year."

"There was sign along the trail," Chantry commented.

"You betchy," the old man muttered. "They'll be blood on the rocks afore we see the last of that outfit. Blood on the rocks for sure."

"Four men?" Chantry suggested.

"Aye. Four of 'em. Mean an' miserable, too. I seen 'em an' got off into the rocks and hunkered down with old Mary here. If they'd a come at me I'd a shot 'em, I would. I never took nothin' from their likes and ain't about to. I'd of hung their hair to dry on a tall pole or a tree somewheres."

"Where are they now?"

"Four, five mile down the mountain and west. I come up the mountain to be rid of them or their breeze. Then I fetched a sight of your fire, and I looked about to see who else was up."

"Did you see anyone else?"

"Ain't that enough for one day? Mister, I been years up and down these mountains, ain't seen nobody. Didn't want to see nobody. I seen a man two year back over on the Animas, an' I reckoned that was enough. Now all to oncet they're a-comin' out of the rocks, all around. Gettin' so a man can't find no peace."

"You better ride high and camp high from now on. That's a bad outfit down yonder."

"You're a-tellin' *me?* I seen 'em."

"You didn't see anyone else? A lone rider, maybe?"

The old man walked up to the fire and speared a rasher of bacon from the pan with his bowie knife. He peered at Chantry from under gray brows. "Was you lookin' for somebody?" he asked, peering.

"I am," Chantry replied. "I'm looking for a girl. And I'd better find her before those down below do. She's who they're hunting for."

"Are they now? Well, why don't you an' me just slip down there 'fore daylight and shoot the four of 'em? Save trouble."

"Shoot them? In cold blood?"

"Cold blood? I don't know if their blood is hot or cold or lukewarm. They're varmints. *Varmints.* I could read their sign and smell their smell. Shoot 'em, says I. Shoot 'em down an' leave 'em for the buzzards. I'd a done it my'self, only one man can't noways get off four shots fast enough. You got you one o' them six-shootin' pistols an' a repeater. Hell, if I had a repeater they be dead by now."

"That's a lovely lady they're chasing," Chantry said. "I'd not want her in their hands."

"Shoot 'em. Stretch their hide. They ain't no good. Not one mother's son of 'em. Shoot 'em, I say."

He ate his bacon and speared another slice. Chantry took up the slab he had and sliced off half a dozen more.

"Seen you huntin' 'em," the old man said, past a mouthful of bacon. "Watched you from up yonder." He gestured toward the high peaks. "Had m' glass on you."

"Glass? You've got a pair of field glasses?"

"Nope. I got me a telyscope. A ginuwine telyscope." He went to his pack and from a roll of blanket extracted a four-foot seaman's telescope of a type Owen Chantry had not seen since he was a boy, and it was an antique then. "With this thing I can see from here to yonder. I was a-watchin' you a-follerin' them. I watched them, too. I seen 'em huntin' that girl. Seen her give 'em the slip."

He demolished the rest of the bacon and wiped the blade of his bowie on his sleeve, then sheathed it. "Come daylight, you an' me an' that girl can meet up. I know a way off this mountain that'll bring us to her before they get there."

"We'd better," Owen said quietly. "That's a bad outfit."

The old man studied him. "You kin to that Chantry feller had the ranch?"

"I am. Did you know him?"

"Know him? I should smile. I knowed him. Why, I rode right up to these mountains with him and

helped lay the timbers of his cabin on the rampart.
I knew him. Good man."

Owen Chantry stared. This gray old man had
known Clive Chantry.

11 Owen Chantry had seen too much to doubt
too much. He was intelligent. He had a healthy vein
of skepticism, but he had traveled too widely and
read too much not to understand that the seemingly
impossible could happen.

As the old man ate and talked, Chantry watched
him thoughtfully. The old man was quick and
active, also very thin, wiry, and strong.

The oldest people Chantry had known all lived at
relatively high altitudes, where many illnesses simply
do not exist because the germs that spread them are
not active in that cold, clear air. Or perhaps there
were simply fewer people to harbor the germs.

"If you know a way to head them off, we'd better
get going early," said Chantry.

The old man looked over his shoulder. "Worried
about her, ain't you? Well, I'd be too. Them as
follers her are a mighty poor lot, a sorry lot."

Chantry pushed a few heavier sticks into the fire,
then stretched out. He was tired . . . he hadn't
realized how tired.

Yet he slept, and well. It was still dark when he
heard the old man breaking sticks. When Owen
raised up, the old fellow glanced over. "Seen you
had coffee," he said. "Ain't had much lately. Git some
chicory in the woods, time to time, but it ain't the
same."

Chantry sat up, shook out his boots carefully to be sure no wanderers had taken shelter there during the night, and tugged them on. He didn't know this old man and prefered to make the coffee himself.

The fire blazed up brightly. Chantry glanced around. It was a perfect camp, sheltered from the wind, partly sheltered from rain, with wood and water.

When he had made coffee and started some bacon, he rolled his bed. The old man went about his business as if alone, taking his horse to water and returning to pack up. Owen did the same, and when they had eaten he kicked earth over the fire. When Owen would have dumped out the coffee, the old man insisted on keeping the grounds, wrapping them carefully in a piece of well-tanned hide.

"Ain't tasted coffee in a spell," he said. "Might be a long time agin. Out here I don't throw nothin' away 'til it's plumb used up."

They started out. The old man led them at a good fast walk down a very steep trail for a hundred yards or so, then at a canter along a gradual slope.

The shot came from afar. A single shot, and then silence. The old man pulled up sharply. Chantry's eyes swept the country in a quick, measuring glance.

All was still. There was no movement, no further sound. The shot seemed to have come from somewhere before them, but in the clear air the sound might have carried for some distance.

Chantry started forward again, the only sound the swishing of the horses' hoofs in the grass. He held his rifle in his right hand, ready for use.

Then right before them, he saw the tracks of several hard-ridden horses. Grass was torn and earth kicked up where the hoofs had dug in. Men riding that hard were going straight to an objective, and not in doubt about it.

Suddenly, half a mile away and racing across a meadow, he saw three riders, two bay horses and a buckskin, running all out.

The old man spoke up suddenly. "Chantry, if I cut out, don't you worry none. I'll be around about."

"Just don't get in the way," Owen replied. "You do what you're of a mind to."

"What you figurin' on?"

"I'm going in and get that girl out of there."

"You see her?"

"No. . . . But look at that rocky knoll yonder? The one covered with aspens. There's been a blowdown hit that slope. See the dead trees? My guess is she's there, trying to make a stand."

"Yeah," the old man said. "They've left one man to pin her down while they try to outflank her. Don't you go gittin' yourself killed. I ain't much hand at goin' agin three, four men single-handed. If'n I was huntin' 'em, now. . . ."

"Hunt them then, but stay out of range. When I go in there I don't want to think about where else my bullets are going."

Chantry walked his horse forward, sitting straight up in the saddle, missing nothing. He was reminded of a time during the war when he was outside Chattanooga. He had led a cavalry charge against a crossroads position, and they had come out of the trees, just like this, unseen by the men in position below.

But this was war of another kind, and he commanded no company. There was only himself and one old man of whom he knew nothing.

He began to trot, his eyes searching for the fourth man.

He heard a shot and saw a puff of smoke from the knoll under the aspens. Almost instantly the hidden marksman replied, and then Chantry saw him, hunkered down behind a mound of earth and brush, lifting his rifle for another shot.

Owen wheeled his horse, the packhorse following, and went in at a dead run.

The man heard him coming too late. Wheeling around, he drew up his rifle for a shot. Yet the turn and the lift of the gun were too fast. The rifle went off before it was fairly lined up, and the next instant Owen rode in up on him, firing with his rifle downward, shooting with one hand.

The man jerked back, spun and dropped. He started to get up and Chantry reined in, turning in a small circle around him.

He'd been hit, all right. Blood stained his shirt and pants right about the beltline on the right side.

"You played hell!" he said.

The man was a rough-looking fellow, but unfrightened.

"You surely bought yourself a ticket!" he said angrily. "The old man will have your scalp for this."

"Does it take four of you to round up one little girl?" Chantry asked.

"Are you Owen Chantry?"

"I am, and that girl is to be left alone. You understand?"

The man spat. "You better tell them yonder. They ain't about to leave her alone. They done had enough of her uppity ways. Who does she think she is?"

"Why don't you ask Mowatt?" Chantry suggested.

The man spat again. "Hell, Mowatt don't know what's good for him. That girl ain't no kin."

The man was clasping his leg tightly, but even as

he talked the initial shock was wearing off. The pain was growing and he squinted his eyes against it, not wanting to let Chantry see.

Out of respect for the man, Chantry turned away. But as he rode off he kept an eye on him to see that he didn't reach for a gun. But the man was wholly concerned with his wound and didn't again look up.

Chantry rode forward, and there were no shots. As he mounted a small knoll he glimpsed Marny's horse, deep inside a clump of trees.

"Marny?" he called softly.

"Come on in," she spoke just loud enough for him to hear. "Although you've come to a poor place."

He rode in through the trees and swung down. She got up from a tangle of fallen logs. There was a smudge on her cheek and the skirt she wore was rumpled.

"Are you all right?" he asked.

"So far, but there's still three more, and they'll be back."

He glanced around quickly. The clump of trees was no more than fifty or sixty feet across, any way you looked, and there were a good many deadfalls and several clumps of boulders. The field of fire in most directions was good.

"They'll come. But when they find out you're not alone, they'll pull out. Then we'll have to run for it."

She glanced at him. "You needn't, you know. I can get along."

She thought again how cold his face was. It was hardboned and strong, but there was little warmth in it until he smiled. There was loneliness in it, too, yet nothing about him invited sympathy. This was a man who had been much alone, with no experience at sharing feelings—probably because there had been nobody to share them with.

"You've always been alone, haven't you?" she asked.

He shrugged, watching the timber across the meadow. "It's better alone than with somebody you don't trust."

"You've never learned to share your feelings."

"Who wants my feelings? A man alone keeps his feelings to himself."

She saw a movement among the leaves. "There's somebody over there."

"I see."

"Are you going to shoot?"

"Not until I see what I'm shooting at. Anybody who shoots blind is a fool. Something moving in the brush may be your best friend. Whenever I squeeze a trigger I know what I'm shooting at."

"But we don't have any friends here!"

"There's Doby. And his Pa. . . . And that old man I met last night."

"Old man?"

"He knows you. He's got a telescope, and there's not much he doesn't know . . . He's also got a Sharps fifty."

"How old is he?"

"Looks like he was here first and they built the mountains around him. But he's spry . . . he's mighty spry, and canny."

There was a yell off to their right, and when Owen turned they were coming . . . all three of them. They were well scattered and coming in at a dead run.

Chantry lifted his rifle like a man shooting ducks, and he fired left, middle, and right.

There was no wasted motion, and no emotion. He just lifted the rifle and came down on his targets, held up the merest second and squeezed off his shots.

The first man veered sharply and dropped his rifle,

then fell down the slope and into the bottom. The second man dropped from the saddle, hit the grass, and lay there. The third wheeled his horse wildly and tried to escape. Chantry let him have three good jumps while he held his fire. Then he shot.

"I held high," he explained, apologetically. "I might have shot through him and killed a good horse."

The horse and rider went racing away across the field, but the man rode limply, one arm dangling.

"Only the horse? Not the man?"

"The man came a-hunting trouble. He rode after a lone woman and he brought plenty of help, so whatever he gets is too good for him. The horse didn't have a choice. He was ridden into this fight, so there's no use for it to suffer." Chantry loaded his rifle again. "If you want to dance, you pay the fiddler. Only in this dance," he smiled at her, "in this dance the devil does the fiddling and you pay in blood."

He glanced around the rocky, tree-covered knoll. "I like this place. When you pick a place to make a stand, you do all right."

The last echoes of the firing had died away. Not the faintest smell of powder smoke remained. It was as if nothing had happened. Only the body lying out there in the grass said otherwise, only a dark patch against the green.

It would still be like this when they were gone. The few scars they left would be erased quietly. Even if left unburied the body would be disposed of in time, and after many years only a few buttons and perhaps a buckle would remain. Men would come, would pass, and where they walked the grass would grow again, and the forest, and there would be no signs of their passing.

"We'd better go," he said. "There's been enough of this."

"They won't stop, you know. Mac Mowatt is losing control. They will want blood now. They'll come after you, Owen, and they'll come after me. But it's the treasure they want."

"Treasure!" he was irritated. "The treasure is out there," he waved a hand. "The treasure is the country itself."

He helped her to the saddle, then mounted and picked up the leadline of his packhorse. They rode out and down across the meadow.

Suddenly the old man came down from a clump of spruces across the way. He rode up to them and reined around, staring angrily at Chantry. "Might o' left me one!" he said. "You cleaned house 'fore I got my fifty up. I d'clare, I never seen such shootin'. You an' me, we could make us a passel out on the buffalo grass."

Owen Chantry led away to the south. He was withdrawn, not wanting to talk. Fighting had been a way of life for as long as he could recall, but he wanted no more of it.

Sensing his mood, Marny said nothing. Against the far-off horizon the Sleeping Ute Mountain bulked large and, nearer, the great shelf of Mesa Verde thrust out, sharp against the sky.

"Do you know what they say?" she spoke suddenly. "We had a half-breed Navajo with us for awhile. He said there were ghost cities up there . . . houses, walls, rooms, all empty and still."

Owen's eyes turned toward the bulk of the great plateau. "Could be," he said, "though it's a less favored place than the mountains we've come from."

The old man disagreed. "Depends on what you're

lookin' for. If you're in a country where there's savage Indians, fighters like the 'Paches and the Navajos, then maybe you want a place you can defend."

Owen Chantry offered no comment. He had been looking far off, and now he drew up on the edge of a slight shelf that offered a good view to the west.

Far off against the sky a slim column of smoke was rising toward the sky. Chantry swore softly, bitterly.

Startled, Marny said, "What is it, Owen?"

"They've fired the ranch," he said. He pointed to the smoke. "It's burning . . . or has been."

"What about the Kernohans?" she asked, suddenly frightened for them.

"I don't know," he said. "I just don't know."

12

Pa was just a-gettin' hitched up when I seen 'em comin'. He had the harness on when I glimpsed the dust on the trail, an' I yelled at him.

"Pa! The Mowatt gang!"

Well, I never seen him act so fast or so sure. I didn't know he had it in him. Pa seemed to me a ord'nary sort of man, and when I picked out heroes he wasn't among 'em. But he wasted no time.

The saddle was already on my horse for I'd been fixin' to take off yonder to the hills. Pa had bound me up tight round the chest and waist, like I was in a cast, and although he didn't know what I aimed to do, he wanted my ribs to knit nice and clean so he done what seemed best to him.

So my horse was ready, an' my rifle was there with extra bullets. An' a bait of grub. An' when Pa seen that dust cloud he run for the house.

I started after him and he yelled back to turn the stock loose. That meant the cows he had up, the one we were milkin', and the heavy stock, so I threw down the corral bars and shied 'em out and into a run down the meadow.

Pa come out with clothes and a few extries. He'd been thinkin' on this. That I figgered out after, 'cause he knew just what to take. He run for the horses.

"Pa!" I yelled. "What about the house?"

"We didn't have a house when we come here, boy, but we did have ourselves and our stock. Let's go!"

We taken out.

The way Pa led off I knowed he wasn't just runnin' wild. He had a bee in his bonnet and soon I seen what it was.

He was ridin' right into Lost Canyon.

Sometime or other he'd found him a trail, and we went for it. Afore we got there, we rode through several big clump of trees, and he done what he could to cover our trail. Then he headed for that place he'd found.

Right where we hit the canyon she probably wasn't much more'n fifteen hundred feet rim to rim, but she was at least five hundred feet deep. And both walls was covered with trees 'cept right at the rim. It was thick cover.

We didn't waste no time. Pa went over that rim and dropped plumb out of sight. When I got that close I seen his horse slidin' on his haunches down a trail that made you catch your breath to look at.

I taken out after him. I wasn't goin' to have Pa sayin' I showed the white feather 'cause of no cliff. But I was sweatin' blue water by the time I'd gone down a hundred feet.

We bottomed out in that there canyon close by a stream, that went rushin' by—a fine trout stream if

ever I seen one, and me with no pole nor no time to
fish.

Sometime or other, Pa had done some scoutin'
without sayin' a word to me about it. He'd been
here afore and he led off almighty fast to a place
where, some time or other, the stream cut back into
the cliff to make of a holler faced off with trees.
Some fallen logs had made a natural corral, and
here we bunched our stock and Pa got down off his
horse.

"You stay here, Doby. I've got somethin' to do up
yonder."

"You goin' back, Pa?"

"They ain't gonna burn that house 'thout me
showin' 'em I disapprove," he said. "I'll just fire a
few rounds and then come on back."

"I'll go along."

"Now, son, you stay here with the stock. I ain't put
in my years raisin' you from a penny-grabbin', candy-
suckin' kid to a growed up man just to see you
killed by no outlaws. You set tight and I'll be back,
and then we'll plan what to do."

"Pa, if'n you raised me to set still and watch my
Pa go into a fight by hisself, you surely wasted your
time. I'm a-goin' with you."

We went up together, me an' Pa, and I never felt
closer to him than right at that time. We went up
together and we run back through the trees. The
Mowatt gang was circlin' round the house, yellin' and
shootin'.

There was smoke from the chimbly, and I guess
they didn't know we was gone. It was too far away
for good shootin', but we had to git back to that
canyon if they took out after us, so Pa hunkered down
among some rocks and he taken a long sight and

squeezed her off. I seen that ol' rifle jump in his hands and one of them horses r'ared up like it was burned and its rider went tumblin'. Then you never seen folks scatter like they done.

But not before I put in some lead. I'd had my eye on one big gent with white suspenders, and I held my sight a mite below where those suspenders crossed on his back, and though it was a good long shot I tightened up the finger until that rifle went off.

I didn't kill him, but I burned him. I made him know he'd been shot at. I sent him a yippin' out of there. But they kept ridin' around. One of 'em throwed a torch at the house that fell on the roof an' rolled off.

Both Pa an' me we opened up an' dusted 'em around with lead. It taken 'em a few shots to realize we weren't inside but outside, and then they turned around and charged at us.

Well, you never seen such a fine sight.

There must've been fourteen or fifteen of 'em an' they was all mounted up on fine horses and they come at us like cavalry chargin'. It was a real sight. A better sight I never saw nor had, lookin' right down the rifle barrel at 'em, and that time when I fired there wasn't no mistake. A man just throwed up his hands and fell off his horse. He hit dust and rolled over and he lay all sprawled out. And Pa took a shot and then he said, "Son, let's get out'n here."

So we taken off.

We taken off a-runnin'. Pa was a better runner than I thought. He was really a-leggin' it when we heard a yell behind.

They'd seen us.

"Here, boy," Pa said. He dropped behind a log and

he hadn't hit dirt 'fore he fired. And me, I was just a hair behind him, firing standin' up behind a good thick tree.

They'd set the house afire. We could see the smoke goin' up.

Them riders split around us and we hightailed it. We was close to the rim then and bullets was kickin' the dust all around us when we went over the rim and flopped down. We was shootin' fast.

They turned right and left into the trees and I started reloadin' and looked over at Pa. And there was blood all over his shirt, and his face had gone white and me, I was scared.

I crawled over to him and slung him over my back, and carryin' both rifles I slid and fell and crawled to the bottom of the canyon. It was no way to handle a hurt man, but I didn't have no choice. I got him to our corral and bathed off his face a little, then tried to peel off his shirt.

I got it off and his undershirt down to his waist. I seen the bullet had hit his shoulder bone and tore through the meat on his shoulder, and down his back a mite. It was pressin' against the skin of his back, a bluelike lump, and I figgered the thing to do was get shut of it. So I slid out my bowie and cut a slit in the skin and the bullet, it just popped out in my hand.

He'd lost some blood. He'd lost a-plenty of blood, but it didn't look to me like no death wound. Still, a body couldn't be sure. So I plugged up the wound with pieces of his undershirt, bathed him off some, and stretched him out.

The bullet hittin' that shoulder bone must have been a shock 'cause he'd passed out, somewheres.

I taken his rifle and reloaded it and set a-watchin' for the Mowatt gang. But didn't none of 'em come.

I was all set for 'em, and I was aimin' to kill me some men. But they never come.

I guess they thought they'd killed us. Or scared us off, or somethin'. Or maybe they didn't relish comin' into that canyon against two rifles that had the drop on them from the trees.

So there I was in the bottom of Lost Canyon, with Pa bad off from lost blood and me not knowin' a thing 'bout what to do.

Time to time, I'd figgered Pa didn't know much. But he was always able to patch up folks or doctor 'em somehow. And me, for all my windy talk, I didn't know what to do.

Right then I surely wasn't thinkin' of no blonde and blue-eyed girls. I was just wishin' I known what to do 'cause there wasn't nobody else around to help.

I kindled us a small fire and started heatin' water in one of the kettles Pa had slung on the horse. I swear, he must have thought it all out ahead of time 'cause he'd took along everything a body might need.

Unpackin' the horses I started rummaging around to see what I could find. I come on a can of white powder Pa had been give by an old man once that was supposed to be good for bob-wire cuts. Now I'd never seen no bob-wire, but I'd heard of it, and a bob-wire cut was a scratch. And this here wound wasn't too different, so when I'd bathed it again, I scattered some of that white powder around it.

Them days, when folks was far from doctors, they just concocted their own medicine, and some of it worked almighty good. I put on the coffeepot and scouted for firewood. And I built our cover a little higher.

For all I knew they might just be a-settin' up there atop the rim waitin' 'til it was sure-enough dark to come at me.

Leavin' Pa for a moment I slipped down and got some water to heat up for broth after I'd made the coffee.

When I got back Pa was stirrin' a mite. How long he'd been bleedin' before I seen he was wounded I don't know. It might have been after the first burst of gunfire, but the way his clothes was soaked up with blood had scared me somethin' awful.

Nobody showed. I guess they never come down off the rim but I wasn't taken no chances going up there. If they nailed me, Pa would be left to die down here. Or tough it out alone.

So I set and waited and listened, longing for *some-body* to come. Only there wasn't nobody goin' to, 'less Owen Chantry come back, and he'd not find us easy, way down in this hole.

I was real scared for Pa and never felt so helpless in all my days.

It was long after midday 'fore Pa opened up his eyes. I was right there with some coffee, and I held the cup for him and let him have a sip or two.

"What happened?" he asked.

"You caught one, Pa. Ain't too bad, but you surely lost blood. You got to sit quiet an' rest. Ain't nobody come. I got the stock took care of and some *dee*fenses built up an' the guns loaded an' I been settin' by just a-waitin' for 'em to come. . . ."

He closed his eyes, then taken a mite more of coffee. It seemed to do him some good, and so I shaved off some jerky into a kettle and stirred it up real good with a fire under it. Soon I'd have us some broth.

"Chantry'll come," he said. "We'll be all right then."

Well, that sort of ired me. "He won't find us, if'n he does. An' even if'n he does come, he'll likely run afoul of them Mowatts. We got to set here til you feel better, then climb up yonder and get out of here."

"This here's our home, boy. We're not goin' to leave. We're goin' back an' build up that house again. I've done wandered all I'm a-goin' to, son. I've been a mover all my born days, but this here's where I intend to stay. Maybe it ain't the finest land, maybe its far from city places, but it's land I can say is mine. We'll stay."

By the time I'd fed him all he would take of that broth, the sun was out of sight and shadows were climbin' the walls of the canyon. I drank what was left.

Then I taken the stock to water and found a patch of open grass along the stream. I dragged some poles into place and made a corral, using rocks, trees, and the side of the canyon. That would keep my stock a-feedin'.

Then I taken up my rifle. "Pa?" I said.

He answered somethin'. Only what he said weren't right. He had him a fever and was wandering in his head. I'd figgered on going up to the rim for a look around.

I was turning back when I noticed the ears on Mary. Mary was a plow horse, and she was a big, powerful brute, but gentle as could be. And she could sense whatever was goin' on around. Mary had her head and ears up. . . . Something was a-comin'.

There wasn't no sound. Not a smidgin. And I listened hard.

Mary's ears were still up, though she seemed less

concerned. Maybe it was a varmint of some kind, a catamount, or the like. I started to set down my rifle when somebody spoke.

"Doby? Is it all right to come in?"

It was that Chantry. It was him, sure 'nough.

"Come on in," I said. I was never so relieved in all my born days. I wasn't alone no longer with nobody to help with Pa but me.

Chantry come out of the trees afoot and stopped there til I had a good look at him. Then he come on up to the fire. He looked at Pa. "How bad is he?"

So I told him. Pa was sleeping, so Chantry said to let him sleep, which was the best doctor of all. But when Pa was awake he'd have a look at the wound. And then he said, "Marny is with me, and an old man."

"An old man?"

"He's been here in these mountains for years. . . . Or so he says."

"I never seen no old man round here. You sure he ain't one of them?"

"He's not. We've been doing some shooting of our own." Chantry went to the edge of the woods and called softly.

They come in. There was that girl, lookin' tired-like but still almighty pretty, and an old, old man who looked like somebody had woke him up from his grave, he was that gray an' old. But he moved about spry enough, an' the way he taken for that coffeepot, you'd a thought he owned it.

"Get some sleep, Doby," Chantry said to me. "I'll look after your pa."

Well . . . I was tired.

They built up the fire some and when I'd stretched out to sleep they set around drinkin' coffee.

Our house had been burned, our stock scattered, an' Pa was wounded. I had me a couple of busted ribs, and there was folks up on the canyon rim that wanted to kill us, but I slept. I just taken off to sleep, and it was full day 'fore my eyes opened up. And there was no more sound than nothin'.

I sat up and looked around. There was Marny Fox, a-settin' by the fire. Pa was a-layin' on the ground not far off, his head on a folded coat.

Chantry was nowhere about.

"Where's Chantry?" I asked.

"He went up to the house."

"Ain't no house. He's wastin' his time. It's done burned down."

"No, it isn't, Doby. The old man looked at it through his telescope and the house is standing. It's been partly burned, all right, but it's still standing."

Course, I should have maybe figgered on that. Heavy timbers like them would take time to burn. A sudden flash fire might not hold long enough to get them tight-fitted, squared-off logs to burnin'.

I went to the creek and splashed water on my face and washed my hands. I taken a mouthful of water and kind of sloshed it around inside, then spit it out. Then I combed my hair with my fingers the best I could.

When I come back to the fire, Marny poured coffee for me. And about that time Owen Chantry come in with that old man who looked like the walkin' dead.

Chantry had an armful of books, some of 'em charred a mite, but that was all. "The house didn't burn, Doby. Only part of the roof and part of the porch."

"You saved you some books," I said. "Is that all you looked for?"

"It's Tennyson I wanted," he said, "I. . . ." A kind of funny look come over his face, and he stared hard at Marny. "Tennyson. . . . Now that *is* a thought."

13 They were huddled together in a bunch.

"I used to read," Marny said, "but we've few books here. If it wasn't for Mac—"

"Mowatt reads?"

"As a matter of fact, he does. My feeling is, considering where he's lived, he's had a better than average education.

"My brother liked Tennyson," Chantry said, "and we had a mutual favorite, a poem called 'Ulysses.'"

It wasn't the right time to be talking of books and poetry. It was time to figure a way to get out of the fix.

The Mowatts had bled and they'd not take it lightly. They'd come back.

"I think we should pay us a visit to Mowatt," said Doby.

"Clive would have his own way of doing things," Chantry mused, "and if he wanted to tell me something he'd have his own way of doing it."

"Them Mowatts got a way of tellin' things, too," Kernohan said, cross-like. "They'll be comin' back and here we set, like an ol' ladies' tea party!"

"You're right, of course," Chantry said. "But I don't think they'll come now. Sooner or later, we must leave this canyon, and when we do it will be easier for them to attack."

Marny brought Chantry a cup of coffee. He took it gratefully and glanced over at Doby.

Chantry knew the younger Kernohan had a chip on his shoulder, and it was probably over Marny. Well . . . that was to be expected. The important thing was not to let it get out of hand. Chantry was, he knew himself, inclined to be impatient, but he must not be impatient with Doby, who was a good lad and had the makings of a man.

Despite his assurances to the others, Chantry also knew the situation was uncertain. How much control could or would be exerted by Mac Mowatt remained to be seen.

He was tired and he needed a shave. Suddenly, he was irritated. Doby was right. It was time to wind this thing up.

"I'm going to see him," he said suddenly.

They looked at him, uncomprehendingly.

"I'm going to see Mac Mowatt and have him call off his dogs."

"You're plumb crazy!" The old man spoke before any of the others could. "They'd kill you afore you got to 'im. An' he ain't callin' nobody off, even if he could."

"We'll see."

Marny was on her feet again. She was wide-eyed and still, staring at him. "They won't listen," she protested. "They'll kill you."

They were right, of course, but he was right, too. Mowatt might see reason. If he did, that would take most of the load off their backs, anyway. Getting to him would be a problem but, despite his normal caution, there was in Owen Chantry a streak of wild Irish rebellion—foolhardiness some would call it. Others would call it plain damn foolishness. . . . But it was his way to bow his neck and plunge in. And better him than the others.

"They won't expect it," he said, more quietly. "I could walk in on them."

"You can walk in," Doby said grimly, "but you'll never walk out again."

In a flash of anger, Chantry spoke and was instantly sorry. "You'd like that, wouldn't you, Doby?"

All their heads came up. Doby flushed. "Nossir, I wouldn't" he said. "You an' me may not see eye to eye, but I'd surely not like to see you get killed. I surely wouldn't."

Doby swallowed.

"Fact is, you go in there an' I'm a-goin' with you," Doby said. "I can shoot, an' I can stand steady. You go in there with me an' you'll see you ain't the on'y one's got hair on his chest."

"I never doubted it, Doby," Chantry said, sincerely. "But I'll have to go by myself. After all," he added, "it was my brother they killed. Whatever it is they're looking for belongs to me."

"Maybe it does," Doby said stubbornly, "an' maybe it don't. It's buried in the ground, or hid. So maybe it's just treasure-trove belongin' to the finder."

Chantry shrugged. "Wherever and whatever it is," he said calmly, "my brother intended me to find it, and so he will have left it."

He wanted it over, done with. He was getting the old urge to get out, to leave. Yet how many times had he done just that? Was that not, in itself, a form of cowardice?

Chantry brushed the wood ashes from his sleeve. He would need a new coat. This one was getting threadbare. He straightened it and walked over to his horse. This was no place to leave his friends, yet. . . . He glanced up the canyon.

He hated to leave. Kernohan was hard hit. Reluctantly, Chantry gave up the idea of moving their camp. They would have to chance it here.

"Sit tight," he said, "I'll go out and take a look."

"If you're goin' after 'em, I'm comin' along," Doby insisted.

"You stay. What about your pa?"

Doby looked trapped, but he argued no longer. "You're takin' a long chance," he said.

Chantry glanced over at Marny. "I'll be back," he said and, touching a spur to his horse, he started for the trail.

He had no certain plan, nor could a plan be devised until he saw the situation at close hand.

It was a good scramble for his horse to get up the trail to the top of the mesa, and Chantry dismounted and led his horse when they reached the crest.

Birds were everywhere about. A squirrel sat on the ground near some rocks.

Every move must be made with caution now, for the renegades who rode with Mowatt were frontiersmen, all of them. His only advantage lay in the fact that they might also be careless.

He walked his horse in the deepest shadows, pausing from time to time to listen. He was disturbed by a vagrant but unfocused notion that kept slipping around at the edge of his mind. Every time he tried to pin the thought into position, to guide it into focus, it slipped away, eluding him.

. . . Something about Tennyson and his brother and himself. They used to write each other letters.

His horse walked softly through the grass and wild flowers that edged the woods. It was the long way around, but he had no desire to trust himself to the open out there, where the distance was shorter.

When he was well away from Lost Canyon, he moved more swiftly.

The air was cool, there was a dampness of dew on the underbrush now. Something stirred and he drew up suddenly. Several shadows moved out into sight. He waited, holding his breath. Then he slowly relaxed. . . . Elk. They liked to feed in high meadows at night.

He caught a faint smell of smoke. He waited, trying to locate the source. The smell faded. He walked his horse on, keeping his eyes on its ears.

The ears were up, and Chantry could sense the interest of his horse. It smelled something too. The smoke, other horses, or men. . . .

A faint breeze stirred the leaves, they rustled, and the breeze passed. He walked on, a few steps further. Chantry had a feeling he was near their camp, but so far he had no definite indication of it.

He caught a gleam through the trees . . . water. He rode closer. It was a small lake, yet he still saw no fire, nor smelled any more smoke. He rode around the lake, taking his time. He glanced at the stars. He still had plenty of darkness before daybreak. Suddenly he caught a whiff of smoke again . . . very faint, but definite.

It seemed to be coming from straight ahead. He kept in the darkest shadows and rode on.

He saw the horses first, felt his own horse swell his sides with a deep breath. "Easy, boy," Chantry whispered. "Take it easy now!" He wanted no whinny that would arouse the camp.

Chantry stepped down from the saddle and with a slipknot tied his horse in the deepest shadows. They were downwind of the Mowatt horses, yet it could be only a few minutes, perhaps a few seconds, until they scented his horse.

He glanced around at the sleeping camp. There was no guard, for obviously they doubted that anyone would have the courage to attack them. Chantry's sense of the fitness of things rebelled at the careless, dirty, ill-kept camp. One by one, he let his eyes slide over the sleeping men until he picked out Mowatt— a bit to one side, an enormous figure of a man covered with a buffalo robe.

Stepping lightly, Chantry walked right through the middle of the camp and squatted on his heels beside Mowatt. It was only then that he realized the old man's eyes were open and on him, and that Mac Mowatt held a pistol in his right hand.

"Mr. Mowatt," he spoke softly.

"Been watchin' you," Mowatt whispered and heaved himself up. "Been watchin' you ever since you showed up . . . listenin' to you come afore that. Got ears like a cat," he said proudly. "Always could hear more'n anybody else."

He rubbed his face, then squinted at Chantry. "You got you a nerve . . . ridin' in here like this. When the boys wake up they'll carve their names in your hide."

"In your own camp?" Chantry acted surprised. "I understood *you* were the man in your outfit. Even an Apache respects an enemy in an Apache's camp. . . ."

"Some Indians do. All right. What d'ya want?"

"Marny tells me that you read."

"*Read?* What in the hell's that got to do with anything? 'Course I read! I had schoolin'. Most of it's been forgot, but I had it. My pa was a reader. Had him a house full. Must have been eight or ten books."

"That's why I came here. I want to talk to you before anybody else gets killed. There is no gold, Mowatt. There never was."

Mowatt snorted. "You 'spect me to believe that? We done heard about this treasure already. How all that gold was brought up from Mexico—"

"'*All that gold?*' Think, man. When my brother came into this country he came out of Mexico with one, maybe two pack mules. He had a small outfit, some grub maybe, and he rode through Apache country. There was no way he could have carried enough gold to matter, even if he had it. And I know enough about him to know that he never cared much for money.

"If he'd had any gold, why would he stop *here?* Where he couldn't use it? Why stop here after riding all that distance out of Mexico?"

"You got you a point there. Always did wonder 'bout that. Figgered he was crazy or a miser or something."

"I believe he brought something with him," Chantry continued, "but I do not think it was treasure. I want to talk to you because you might understand, you might grasp the idea . . . which I am sure they," Chantry gestured at the camp, "would not.

"Although," he added, "Frank Mowatt might." Chantry looked straight at Mac Mowatt. "You know, Mr. Mowatt, Frank is the best of the lot. He'll stay by you because he's loyal and a good son. But he's the only one of you who's worth a tinker's dam, and that includes you."

Mowatt stared at him. "You got you a nerve. Talkin' that way to Mac Mowatt."

Even Chantry was amazed at what he'd said.

"I had nerve when I rode in here, and whether you believe it or not, I'll ride out, too. But I thought maybe I could talk some sense into you. You've got a tough bunch of boys here, but you'll waste them trying for something that would keep the least of you in whiskey for less than an hour. Believe me."

"You know what it is?"

"No . . . but I've a hunch. My brother was interested in the old civilization of Mexico. He was a thoughtful, intelligent man. Most of us Chantrys have gone off wandering for no special reason, but when he went to Mexico and Central America, I think it was for a special purpose. And I think he found something down there that has some bearing on history."

Chantry paused. "He never cared much for money, and he passed up a dozen chances to have an easy life. All he ever wanted was to see what lay over the horizon, to study the ways of man."

"Maybe." Mowatt hitched himself around and reached for a boot. "Did you ride in here just to tell me that?"

"No." The two were moving quietly away from the camp. "I wanted to talk some sense into you. I have nothing against you. So why should I kill you? Or any of your outfit? I came into this country to stay. I'm going to hang up my guns and do some ranching."

"You?" Mowatt was skeptical. "I'd have to see that to b'lieve it."

"You should do the same thing, Mowatt. Get yourself some land while you can, settle down and raise cattle." Chantry paused. He had to say it. "The real reason I came into camp tonight was because of Marny."

"Marny?" The old man's face turned toward him. "She's got nothing to do with you. Don't bring Marny into this."

"She has everything to do with it. I had to shoot a couple of your boys yesterday. They'd chased her over a dozen miles of country. I killed one of them and put lead into three others."

"Marny? My boys? You lie, Chantry!"

His voice was choked up.

Finally, he said, "What do you know about Marny?"

"That she's a fine, beautiful young woman who respects and loves you, despises your outfit, and deserves a better chance. In fact, that's the real reason I rode in here tonight. You're her stepfather. I want to ask Marny to marry me. And I want your permission."

14   "You *what?*"

"You're her oldest living relative. I suppose that legally you're her guardian. So I came to you."

"Well, of all the damn gall! You—!" Mowatt stared at Chantry, then began to chuckle. "I'll be a yeller-livered coyote if that don't take first prize! You ridin' in here with my boys huntin' your hide, just to tell me that!"

"She's a lady," Chantry continued quietly, "and somewhere under that tough old hide of yours there used to be a gentleman. A man who knows how things should be done."

"You said anything to her 'bout this?"

"No. . . . She'd be surprised. She might even laugh at me. But I had to do it."

"Well, I'll be damned," Mac Mowatt threw his cigar butt into the ground and rubbed it out with his toe. "You'd think we was back in Richmond or Charleston or somewheres like that." He shook his head. "No . . . you're a gunfighting drifter, Chantry."

"It would take a gunfighter to get her out of this. You've lost your control. I—"

"Lost my control? Like hell, I have! I can—"

"I told you I was settling down. I'm going to ranch, if you'll put your outfit off my back."

"What do you mean, I've lost control?"

"Well, they went out after her, didn't they? Said she was uppity, that they'd just show her."

"I hope you killed that man."

"He took one in the leg that didn't do him any good, and so far as I know he's still out there."

Then Owen Chantry got to his feet. "Now you know, Mac Mowatt. I want to court Marny, and I've come to you as a gentleman should. You call off your boys, or there's going to be war."

"How long do you think you'd last?" Mac Mowatt had risen too.

"Jake Strawn is trouble."

"And Tom Freka?"

"I thought he was leading the chase after Marny. I'm pretty sure he's killed at least one woman. Get him out of the country or I'll kill him."

Mac Mowatt rubbed his hand over his face. "Damnit, Chantry, I like you! Damned if I don't. You shape up like a man. But I've got these boys. And when you lead an outfit like this you got to *lead*. You got to stay ahead of them. I dunno . . . I really dunno. Why don't you and Marny light out? There's a preacher in the San Luis valley, and there's always Santa Fe."

"This is my country, Mowatt. I've come home. If your boys want war, they'll get it. My advice to you is to latch onto Strawn. He and your son Frank are *men*."

Mowatt shrugged. His mind was made up. "You an' them farmers don't count for much, Chantry. Those boys will cut you down."

"Then it's war?"

"It is," Mowatt said. "But I'll say this Chantry, if you pull through somehow, and Marny wants you for her man, you've got my permission. If it plays that way, Chantry, give her a good life. She's a mighty fine young woman."

Chantry turned and walked into the trees. He had gained nothing.

He worked his way back toward his horse, moving slowly, taking every precaution. Twice he paused to listen . . . ready for an instant shot.

He caught the vague glisten of moonlight on the polished leather of his saddle and heard the black shift its hoofs. Something moved in the shade and a low voice said, "I always wanted to kill me a big man, one o' them special fightin' men. I always figgered they was just so much talk. You know who this is, Chantry? This here is Thrasher Baynes, an' I got you dead t' rights!"

Chantry felt suddenly very tired. Almost bored. Would they never learn? He wanted to kill no one. He had never wanted to kill. He had fought in wars, he had fought in the service of the law, but he had never, even as a boy, wanted to be known as a killer of men.

Thrasher Baynes stood in the darkness. Thrasher Baynes had spotted him. He was expecting Chantry to reply, and he needed that reply to know exactly where he was.

Owen Chantry waited, alert to the slightest sound. If Thrasher moved. . . . On his own right Chantry had a tree, on his left an open space some six feet across. And beyond that, his horse.

Thrasher spoke again. This time his voice was a tone higher. "What's the matter, Chantry? You scared? You too scared to talk? I'm a-gonna kill you, Chantry."

Chantry didn't move. His rifle was on that voice, his finger on the trigger, the slack taken up. . . . He was only a hair from firing a shot, and he knew when he fired he would fire three times—one right down the middle, one somewhat lower right, and a third to the left.

If his first shot scored and Thrasher started to fall, Chantry'd have a good chance of nailing him a second time.

"Yaller, ain't you?"

They would all be coming now. It was only a matter of time.

Chantry fired into the sound. Fired once, then as fast as he could work the lever, twice more. Then he walked to his horse, pulled the slipknot, and climbed into the saddle.

Behind him something groaned and thrashed about on the ground. Then all was silent.

Owen Chantry knew where the trail was and how it lay. He went down it at a dead run. He had done what had to be done. What happened now would be on their own heads. He had had no hope of talking them out of their battle. That would have been asking too much of human nature. Yet now Mac Mowatt had been told of the growing lack of discipline in his own gang.

He slowed his pace among the trees, but rode steadily onward. The air was cool, the light wind from off the mountains chilly. Bright moonlight bathed the trail.

He had asked for a girl's hand in marriage before he had even asked the girl, or even talked to her of love. Was he a fool? Could she, or any woman, love him?

Was he the kind of man who would make a fit husband for Marny Fox . . . if he lived?

He had declared war. And although he might have help, it was a one-man war. They had killed his brother. It was his own land over which they were fighting. What his brother had left was his legacy, whether it was wealth or knowledge or a dream.

The ranch house had not burned down. Its timbers were solid, allowing no air holes. Some had just charred. A part of the roof had burned, but a late afternoon shower—usual in these mountains—had put out the fire. Nothing a good man with tools couldn't repair in a few days, and clean up in a week.

However, the place was exposed. They could not return there yet.

They'd come after him, the Mowatt gang. He dismounted and led his horse to water. Some distance away, he stretched out on the grass with his saddle for a pillow and watched the declining moon.

He dozed, awakened to listen, and dozed again. He knew all the sounds of the night and what they meant, and his horse was alert as only a former wild horse is, having lived too long with danger.

The nights when he slept through without awakening were few. He had taught himself to awaken at the slightest change in sound or air.

When the sky was gray and the landscape still black, he got up, sat on a log, and tugged on his boots, stamping his feet to settle them well. He led his horse to water again, saddled up, and considered what lay before him.

To kill every one of the gang might be necessary, but he had no wish for such an end. Yet he was one man alone, and the enemy was many. And victory would mean life for others than himself.

He thought about these things ruefully. The only gallant and dashing thing about him at the moment was the fine black horse he rode.

When he reached the house, he gathered a few half-burned rags and wrapped them up with string, the coarse twine Kernohan used to tie up bundles of corn.

Then Owen Chantry mounted the black horse and rode into battle. There were no banners flying, but the Irish were accustomed to fighting gallantly for causes already lost.

He was riding forth to battle. And his only weapons were wit and the bitter wine of his experience.

15 On his long night ride back from the ranch house, Owen Chantry had crossed Turkey Creek Canyon and turned west along the south rim, scouting it all the way to Lost Canyon.

If they followed his trail, they would ride where he had ridden. . . . And they *would* ride his trail, because otherwise they might lose him.

In a patch of woods overlooking his trail, but several hundred yards off, he dismounted. He caressed the black and talked to it. The horse turned its head and pushed at Chantry with its nose.

The grass along these trails and back in the cul-de-sac was tall and dryer than elsewhere. There was sparse timber. He glanced at the sky. It was scattered with the usual white puffballs of cloud. By midafternoon they would bunch up and there would probably be rain.

He knew a way to box them in.

He saw their dust before he saw them. Just a thin trail rising up from the dry grass. He walked back to his horse, took up the reins, and mounted. They were following his trail, just as he intended.

Putting a finger in his mouth he wetted it well and held it up. The wind was from the east, toward Lost Canyon. They'd have a little trouble at the canyon's rim because there was a shelf of rock there, bare rock, and the trail would be lost for a little way.

When they had gone on by he rode down toward them. He would have to be quick, for the ride into and out of the cul-de-sac would be no more than a mile.

He drew up when he'd cut their trail and glanced along a line toward a smaller canyon. Then he struck a light and lighted a bundle he'd made of dry cloth and grass. The bundle was big, and took longer than he liked to flame up. Then he got into the saddle and took a turn around the pommel with the other end of the twine. He walked his horse west, dragging the burning bundle. Behind him the grass caught fire and began to burn toward the rim. The wind was not strong enough, but it was there, and the fire would generate wind of its own.

He walked the black along, and first the grass began to burn, then the brush. He started to trot his horse and rode up to the other canyon rim. Then he loosed the twine and turned away, riding swiftly. A half mile off, he glanced back. Smoke was billowing up, and he saw a sudden arrow of fire as a tree loaded with sap exploded into flame.

He knew he wasn't going to burn them. They were

too smart for that. They would find a gap in the line where the fire had not taken hold, or they would ride into the small lake near the rim. What he wanted to do was worry them, make them wonder what was coming next. He wanted them to know it wasn't going to be easy for them. He wanted them to think about losing, about coming up with nothing for all their trouble, about dying. He wanted them to sweat. He wanted them to get so disgusted they'd quit.

He trotted the black, watching for the home trail. He had no fear of the fire burning over into Lost Canyon because of that strip of bare rock.

I was puttin' sticks on the fire when I seen him coming down from the rim. Seems like no matter how long he'd been ridin' or where, he always sat his saddle like he was on parade. It bothered me some, but at the same time I envied him. He surely was a fine-looking man, even if he was wore out a little around the edges.

"You smell that smoke?" I asked him.

"Nothing to worry about, Doby. It'll burn out in a few more minutes."

Marny came up from the stream, brushing her hair as she walked. The gladness in her eyes worried me more than Chantry. What did she see in him, old as he was?

"How's Kernohan?" Chantry asked.

"He's better. He's had some soup and he drank some more coffee. I think he's gaining a little." She looked at him, his face haggard in the morning light. "Have you slept at all, Owen?"

Calling him by his first name like that!

"Enough. But if there's anything to eat. . . ."

"It's ready."

"Where's the old man?"

"He's disappeared into the timber."

Trees shaded the ground, but there were spots of sunlight. Chantry ate a bit, then sat down under a tree, his rifle across his lap. He weren't never far from that rifle. And sleepy he might be, but when he woke up he was ready.

Marny came up with a refill for his coffee, but he had his head back, plumb asleep. "He looks beat," I commented. "Ridin' all night, likely. I'd give a coon to know what he's been up to."

"I am glad he's back with us," Marny said. "Between the two of you and the old man—"

"I don't cotton to that old man. Says he's been around since Noah's ark, but I never seen him before. I don't know what he's up to, but I don't like it no how . . . or him either."

"Has he told you his name?"

"He's mentioned a couple, but I don't believe either one of 'em is right. He sorta smiled when he told me. Likely he don't even remember. I don't believe he's been here long. We woulda seen him."

"Doby? How many bears have you seen in these mountains?"

"Ain't seen any. Nor cougars, neither, but they're around here."

"That's right."

Well, I taken another look at her. "I see what you mean," I admitted, "you figger he's like them. If I ain't seen a bear or a cougar, that don't mean they ain't here."

She went over to where Pa lay. His eyes opened and he looked up at her. His mind wasn't wanderin' this morning and he seemed better, like she'd said. I was never no hand with sick folks and was uncomfortable bein' around 'em, because I never known what to do. Ever' once in a while I figgered to ask Pa what a body did at them times, and I kept telling myself to listen and watch other folks. Womenfolks, they just seemed to know. But how, I never could figger out. Just come natural to 'em, I reckon.

I taken my rifle and edged out toward the creek to where I could listen, but the creek was so noisy itself I couldn't hear much. Yet I worked upstream about half a mile, but I couldn't see nothin' except plenty of trout in the stream. And when I got back to camp, Chantry was awake and cleaning his guns. I never did see a man fuss so much over guns. Them guns and his horse. I said somethin' about it, and he looked up at me.

"We live by them, Doby. A man without a gun and a horse in this country is downright helpless. You take care of them, and they'll take care of you."

'Course that made sense, but it was a mighty lot of fussing to do, seemed to me. Pa was always after me, too. Couldn't bear to see a used gun set down without cleaning.

The old man come back then, and he was chucklin'. He filled his cup with coffee and kept looking at Chantry, chuckling some more. "You sure played hob," he said. "You surely did. That outfit is fit to be tied. Run 'em all into the lake, you did, an' some of 'em got in up to their ears. You fairly trapped 'em."

Well, when we asked him he told us about Chantry catchin' them with a grass fire.

"Taken a shot at 'em m'self," the old man said, "just to bugger 'em a mite. I was a mite far off for good shootin', but I burned one of 'em. Burned him good . . . dropped his rifle an' he taken off. He come

137

back for his rifle after awhile, but somebody'd snuck down there an' packed it, packed it right off."

"Good!" Chantry smiled. "A man doesn't find a rifle every day."

He surely didn't, and I felt sorry for the man who lost it, at the same time thinkin' it was one more we wouldn't have to worry about aimin' at us.

Chantry kept sizing up the old man and finally he asked him when he come into the country. That old man, he canted his head and his old eyes twinkled. He gulped down some more hot coffee an' he says, "I don't pay no mind to years. Ain't seen a clock or a calendar since I was a boy. But this here much I'll say. When I first come over on the dry side I already had hair on m' chest. I was fit to handle m'self or anybody that come to catch me. Only nobody come."

"But you knew Clive?"

"I knowed him. Had his head in a book most o' the time. But he was a good man for all of that . . . a good man. Kept the coffee on . . . never had to wait in his house. Rode with Clive once. Down in Mexico with another feller named Mowatt. But we got chased out. They ran us awhile, but one of Clive's friends was an Otomi Indian. He knowed the country, an' he taken us out.

"We had us a fight an' the Indian was killed, but 'fore he died he tol' Clive 'bout some papers. He'd seen him readin', so he told him his people had papers, too. Told him where they was hidden. . . . Old papers, and carvin's and such.

"Clive, he'd have it no way but to go lookin', an' sure enough he found 'em. Wasn't all he found, neither. He found a heap of grief and trouble.

"Clive Chantry was the one built the cabin on the rampart. And buried or hid whatever it was."

"How much gold did he have?" I put in.

The old man chuckled. "Gold? Laddie, you'd of had a hard time fillin' a thimble! I know! I was there! We three had us some gold until the big fight in Mexico, an' then we was lucky to get out with our skins! We had us some horses and two mules, an' we had some grub. We had powder an' lead, an' mighty little else. Gold? I should smile!"

Well, there it was! Unless this old man was a-lyin', or had found where the gold was hid and had it hid someplace hisself. I taken another look at him. Old he might be, but he was no damn fool. He was smart as a hill-country fox.

"I never heard of no Otomi Indians," I muttered.

"There are many tribes in Mexico," Chantry said, "with many languages. I know nothing of the Otomis either, except that I've heard their language is very different, with no kinship to the other Indian tongues. Of course, that may be just hearsay."

"That Otomi was a good man," the old man said, "but he was a drifter and a wanderer, never stayed put nowheres."

"I still believe there was gold," I declared. "Or gems and such. I don't see why a man would waste his time totin' old papers or whatever all the way from Mexico. What I want to know is where it was hid?"

The old man shrugged. "Who knows? Clive was mysterious. Wherever he hid the stuff, nobody ever knowed. You'll play hob findin' it."

Chantry went off under a tree and rolled up in his blankets, and the old man, he just set awhile staring into the coals of the fire an' talkin' to hisself. I taken my rifle an' started scoutin' out again up toward the rim. When I finally got there I set down amongst the rocks and brush where I could see, and I started watchin' the trails.

That was a mean outfit and I didn't trust them no way at all. Chantry said he'd talked to Mac Mowatt, but I didn't know whether to believe him or not. I didn't figger anybody could walk right into an outlaw camp and talk to the leader without getting killed. But maybe he done it.

I couldn't figure that old man out either. It was hard to believe he'd lived in that country so long and we never even seen him. Yet it could be so. It was right what Marny said about bears and lions, and if they could do it maybe a man could too. It made a body downright uneasy to think there's folks around, peerin' at him without him knowin'. Made me look around.

Settin' there like that, nothin' on my mind, thoughts kept edging their way up front, thoughts I'd put out no welcome for. It kept nagging at me there might be men who set such store by papers they'd risk their lives to save 'em. That was a new thing to me.

Shifting my rifle, I squinted down the trail. No dust. No smoke. Yet somethin' about that trail worried me.

I oughta be thinking of meat, too. We didn't have much left. Maybe some fish. I could rig myself up a pole and catch a bait of mountain river trout, be mighty tasty.

I taken another sight down trail and still seen nothin'. I studied the country round, then backed out the brush and went down the trail to the Lost Canyon camp.

Owen Chantry was polishin' his boots when I got there. "See anything, Doby?" he asked.

"All quiet," I told him. "What you reckon they're figurin' on?"

"If they're smart, they're pulling out about now. But I don't think they're that smart, or that willing to believe they've wasted their time. What they should do, not being smart enough to quit, is to hole up and hide out until I've found whatever it is they think is so valuable."

"Might be a long time," I said, thinking about that. For how could any man alive read the thoughts of a man long dead? There were miles of country in which to hide something, clefts in the rock, hollow trees, boulders, places where holes could be dug. An' I said so.

Chantry agreed. "Clive knew me, and I knew him. He would think of something, some clue we would both understand. But whatever it is, I can't figure it out from here. I've got to go back to the cabin. I have to be where he was and try to think his thoughts."

"However could you do that?" Marny asked.

Chantry put down the cloth he'd been using to polish his boots. "Put myself in his place. He may have known they would try to kill him."

Marny flushed. "I had no idea they'd kill him. You see, they thought whatever it was was in the house . . . the ranch house. I thought so, too."

"So?" Owen Chantry was lookin' right at her, kinda cold and steady.

"They told me they were going to kill him if he didn't tell them where it was, and I begged them not to. I'd met him, you see, while riding. We'd talked. . . . He was much older. . . . He seemed much older than you, Owen. I liked him. He was a gentleman. And after being with them. . . . Oh, I liked it! I liked being treated like a lady, I liked listening to him. I was anxious to learn things. How to be a lady, how to act, what women wore. Clive seemed to know something about everything. Then they told me they were going to kill him, so I begged them to let me try to find it. They agreed.

"So I went down. I told Clive I'd run away, that I was afraid of them, and that much was almost true. I *wanted* to run away, but I was always afraid . . . always.

"He let me stay there. He told me he'd protect me until he could figure out how to get me away safely. And when he was out of the house, I looked for treasure. The only thing I ever discovered was that it could not possibly be hidden in the ranch house.

"We used to talk a lot. Suddenly he'd seem very lonely. And most of all, Owen, he talked of you. He'd read poetry to me, and to himself, and he read other things. And when I realized he had nothing of value hidden in the house, I went to them and tried to tell them. I begged them, pleaded with them but they wouldn't listen. They thought he'd made a fool of me.

"Finally, Mac promised they'd do nothing. Or I thought he'd promised, at least. And then they killed him. And ransacked the house, and found nothing . . . nothing.

"And he was dead. Clive Chantry was dead."

16 Mac Mowatt sat hunched on the butt end of a log in Hell's Hole, a small hollow on the course of the middle fork of the range. Above him, the great bulk of the hogback loomed, rising over a thousand feet to its crest.

It was not a good campsite and Mowatt was not in a good mood. He stared gloomily into the flames, Owen Chantry's words of the night before sticking like spurs into his brain.

Suppose Chantry was telling the truth. Suppose all this searching was for nothing at all. Suppose all this waiting, all this grief, plus the loss of several good men, and the trouble they were in now was in vain.

All of them had reached the lake before the flames burned anyone bad, but several had been singed and were suffering. A burning leaf had set Ollie Fenelon's hair afire before he could slap it out, and he had a raw scalp. And Tom Freka's big horse had a burn across his hip from a bullet that had come out of nowhere.

His own clothes were still damp from the soaking, for most of them had gone in up to their necks. Their blanket-rolls were wet, and a lot of their grub had been soaked. Pierce Mowatt, his half-brother and the best cook among them, was contriving something at the fire. Several coffeepots were on the coals, and things might soon be looking better.

"I'll kill him!" Freka yelled suddenly. "I'll break both his legs and show him what the feel of fire is!"

Jake Strawn rolled the tobacco in his jaws and spat. "You get a chance to kill him, you better not try no fancy touches."

"You think he's really somethin', don't you?" Freka sneered.

"Uh-huh. He's the best I ever seen . . . unless it's me," Strawn was complacent. "He's right handy, an' you choose your weapon. Knife, pistol, or club, he's rough an' randy."

"I'll kill him!" Freka repeated.

"Pa?" It was Frank, and Mac Mowatt looked up.

"I'm takin' a ride to Santa Fe. Maybe El Paso. I'd be pleased not to ride alone."

There was a momentary silence, then Mac shifted his boots. "Don't talk that way, Frank. We need you here."

"I got no liking for this dodging about in the brush, all on somebody's say-so that there's gold." So much was what Frank thought and felt. When he continued, he was speaking partly to affect the others. "I want to see a woman. I want some lights and some fancy grub. Or at least some grub we don't have to fix for ourselves. There's stages down near the border. And there's cattle can be stole across the border an' sold this side. An' vice versa. We're a-wastin time here, Pa."

"There's got to be a mint o' gold," Mac said. "Why, they was comin' out of Mexico with an army after 'em! What was they after 'em for? Just those fool papers Clive was supposed to have?"

"Who told you about that army, Pa?" Frank inquired mildly. "That's just border talk, you know that. An' if they had any gold, why didn't they spend it? Why would a man bury gold in the ground? Did we ever bury any of ours?"

"Why should we bury it?" Pierce asked.

"That's what I'm saying," Frank said quietly. "Why should anybody bury gold? If there's a posse after 'em and they need to lighten their load, maybe. If they got so much they can't carry it, maybe. But if there was an army after Ben Mowatt and Clive Chantry, what happened to the army?"

Fenelon looked up. "Whad'ya mean?"

"They were after them, weren't they? This was Spanish territory them days, wasn't it? So if they was after them, why did they stop short? Mowatt got killed, and Clive settled down right here an' stayed, so they wouldn't have had no trouble findin' him."

"Aw, hell!" Fenelon said. "We know an army chased 'em! Why, Charlie Abrams down to Socorro, he knowed all about it. He said they was Mex soldiers, and he was on the border when they was chasing Mowatt an' Chantry."

"Wasn't any border," Frank said quietly. "Not them days. I heard tell Charlie never even come into this country 'til just before the war."

He got out his pipe and loaded it. He didn't want to talk anymore. They were out-of-sorts and sore at the world. Let them stew about it.

Treasure! Lost mines! How many stories had he heard? Some of them made sense. Some of them had some basic logic behind them, but most of them wouldn't hold water.

He got up and started for the river bank. He'd taken no more than a step when he heard the rumble. He started to turn, saw what was happening and yelled, "Run! Rockslide! *Run!*"

They ran. They scattered. Somebody charged into Frank full-tilt and they both fell, sprawling on the ground just in time to be missed by a boulder the size of a mule. It hit a rock above them and bounded over their heads. Men were falling, cursing. Somebody screamed. There was a roaring behind them, then a few scattered rocks falling down, a trickle of pebbles, and silence.

And then the swearing began.

"Help!" a voice called. "I got a busted leg!"

Men came out of the creek, stamping the water from their legs, pausing to empty their boots.

"Where's the horses?" Mac Mowatt yelled. There was more cursing.

145

"Gone, god damnit!" Pierce said.

Their fire was out, buried under a deluge of rocks and gravel. Their coffeepots were spilled, smashed, or buried. Their food was under a heap of rocky debris from off the cliff.

It hadn't been a big slide, but big enough to frighten the horses, wipe out their camp, and ruin their supper.

"Now why in hell," Pierce muttered, "did that have to happen?"

"Happen, hell!" Ollie Fenelon shouted. "That didn't *happen!* It was done! Somebody had to start that rockslide!"

Mowatt swore, and Freka said again, "I'll kill him, damnit. I'll kill him!"

Jake Strawn gathered up what he could find of the camp gear. When Frank came over to help, Strawn said, "El Paso sounds better'n better."

Strawn found one dented but intact pot, and they found most of their gear and bedding, after some digging. One rifle had a broken stock, and the wooden stirrup on a saddle was broken. But that could be repaired, and the gun stock also, with time.

When the coffee was ready they took turns, for they needed more than one pot. It was a slow, tiring supper they ate and finally, on ground a hundred yards from their original campsite, they bedded down.

It was after midnight before the camp was quiet. Within the hour that followed, all were asleep. Even Mac, who'd been doing some serious thinking.

The moon rose later and finally shone into the canyon. Suddenly the perfect stillness of the mountain night was split wide open by the heavy explosion of a rifle shot, unnaturally loud in the quiet.

Tom Freka came to his feet with a scream of pure

fury, and as he lunged erect a bullet hit the ground within inches of his toes. He sprang back, tripping over Frank Mowatt to fall in a heap. Another shot followed, and then stillness.

Bleary-eyed from weariness, only half-awake, the men stared around, and then from the cliff above them came a mocking voice, singing, "We're tenting tonight on the old campgrounds, give us a song to cheer—"

Tom Freka emptied his rifle toward the sound high above.

"Goodnight, boys!" It was Owen Chantry's voice. "Sleep late in the morning."

Wiley swore bitterly, and after a minute or two they rolled in their blankets. But it was a long time before they could sleep. Pierce Mowatt came out of the darkness and walked down by the stream, lighting his pipe, half-expecting a shot. But no more shots were heard.

The trouble was, Mac Mowatt reflected, now they would never know. Nobody would strike a match, try to make coffee, or settle down for a meal without wondering when the shots were going to come.

There were two possible solutions: leave the country or track down Owen Chantry and kill him. He said as much to Freka.

"There's another," Freka said. "I think he's got a case on Marny. If'n we could get Marny back, he'd come for her."

"No!" Mowatt's voice was flat and harsh. "Marny's kin. Keep her out of this."

"It's your funeral," Freka said, but he was doing his own thinking. If he could get Marny, then he'd have Marny and he could get Chantry at the same time. Bait him right into a trap . . . a juicy trap.

Jake Strawn—big, tough, and raw-boned, a gun-hand in many a cattle war, a man who'd done time in two prisons—looked across at Freka. Tom Freka might be a mystery to some, but he was an open book to Strawn. Jake turned on his side with disgust and closed his eyes. The trouble with being on the wrong side of the law was the kind of company you had to keep.

Daylight came to the camp on Lost Canyon with a red glow on the rimrock. Owen Chantry, who had slept two hours, went down to the river and bathed his face in the cold water, cupping it in his hands to dash into his eyes. He stood up, shaking water from his fingers. The trouble with doing what he had done was that the other side could do it too.

It was time to move. Kernohan was better and might be strong enough to sit a horse, if they didn't have to go too far. Chantry watched a squirrel run out on the rocks near the water, then turned back to the camp.

He was tired, dog tired, and it was catching up with him. Yet he knew he could go for days . . . might have to go for days.

"Ten," he said aloud. "Ten, eleven, twelve—" What had Clive been trying to say? The other day he'd again had a fleeting idea that had disappeared as quickly as it came . . . some haunting thought that had come to him.

He walked back to the camp and sat down. Marny was up and combing her hair. The filtered sunlight caught the light in it, and Chantry watched. She was uncommonly graceful, her every move.

"Nice morning," he said quietly.

"Where were you last night? I was worried."

He chuckled softly, amused. "I went serenading. I wanted to sing those boys to sleep."

She stared at him, not knowing what he meant. He picked up the book of poetry and turned the pages under his thumb. Clive had read it a lot. "Locksley Hall" had been a favorite of his and Clive's too. There was a copy of "Marmion" by Sir Walter Scott, tucked in the pages, written in Clive's own hand. It gave him a sudden pang of loneliness. He would never see Clive again.

Suddenly, he knew. Suddenly Owen believed he knew where Clive Chantry's treasure was hidden.

17 At least he had a clue. Even with the clue, it would take some searching to find. But at least he now knew how Clive was thinking.

Clive Chantry had been a considerable scholar, yet he had taken his linguistic skills casually, learning several languages before he was fifteen, and acquiring others as the need developed or as his interests demanded. In several years of wandering, much of it in South and Central America as well as Mexico, he had mastered several Indian tongues.

Although not pretending to be a scholar, he was keenly aware of the demands of scholarship, and his wanderings had taken him into places, and brought him into contact with people, who were relatively unknown.

There might actually be a treasure.

Owen Chantry watched Marny brush her hair but, attractive as she was, his thoughts were far away.

Mac Mowatt would not take the midnight attack on his camp lying down. He dare not, if he expected to lead his outfit. They would be angry, eager to retaliate. And this time they would come in for the kill with no nonsense about it.

"We've got to move," Chantry said, suddenly.

"Move to where?" Doby said. He was sitting quiet with his thoughts. "All we're gonna do is get out in the open where they can wipe us out."

Chantry glanced at the old man, who was leaning on his rifle, watching them with his bright-gray eyes. "You know this country best. Is there a good hide-out nearby?"

"A couple. Figgered you'd be wantin' to go back to the cabin on the rampart. There's places up there—"

"How about water?" Doby protested. "I seen no water." At least if he had, he didn't remember it.

The old man chuckled. "You youngsters, you never look. Got no *eyes!* Why, there's a passel o' water right near to the door! Off there to the right, hid behind the brush. Ol' Clive, he was no fool! A man needs water, an' he built hisself a dam. Across the gully to catch the runoff. Got a drain for her, too, an' a rock to stop off the drain when need be, so's the water keeps fresh.

"Rained there t'other night, so there'll be water . . . maybe five hundred gallons . . . maybe twice that much."

"I don't want to get Pa stuck in no cabin. You can't get out up there, an' you're caught in a trap."

"No need, son. Chantry, you're an army man. Move out from the cabin, set up a perimeter defense. Give y'rself room to move in. Why, there's a-places up there a good man with a rifle could stand off an army! I can show y' where. Now, if y' really—"

"I do," Chantry said bluntly. "Let's go!"

Within a matter of minutes they were moving, with the old man to ride point, followed by Marny and Kernohan, then Doby, with Owen Chantry riding well back to cover their flight, if need should be.

"Wrong time o' day," the old man grumbled. "Of a nighttime I could take y' there easy as pie. This here way we got t' keep under cover, got t' ride careful, like."

"We can hole up somewhere on the way," Chantry said. "Just get us away from here!"

The old man spat, shifted his rifle in his hands, and then said. "Got just the place! Take 'em awhile t' find us there!"

"How far?"

"Four, five mile. 'Bout that." He pointed with a long bony finger. "South."

He led off down canyon. Curiously, the canyon's walls grew less steep, and the canyon itself flattened out into a series of meadows. The old man skirted a low hill, then led them up the slight bank and into the trees.

Chantry rode behind, rifle in hand. He was worried. They had left the canyon almost too easily, and his every sense told him trouble was near, though the old man was wily. The way he had taken them was hidden from view, and there was a chance they'd escaped observation.

The day was hot and still. And it was quiet, altogether too quiet. He trotted his horse to catch up. Doby was leading the packhorses, including his own buckskin.

How many were left in Mowatt's crowd? Several had been killed, although he could be certain of only a few . . . three, perhaps. And several injured.

Chantry ducked his head under a low branch, glimpsed Doby ahead with the packhorses and at a bend in the trail, he watched Marny's red hair catch the sun. Not really red, but when the sun caught it—

He heard the faintest of sounds and turned sharply in the saddle.

Nothing. . . .

Had it been some animal or bird? Or a branch stirred by the wind? Entering a thick grove, he drew up to look back again. . . . There was nothing.

He cantered his black across a small meadow and glanced around again.

Where was the old man taking them? They had been traveling slowly to take advantage of every bit of cover, and they must have covered three or four miles. Now they were leaving the cover behind, the best of it, at least. The trees were mostly cedars now, some piñon pines. This country was broken and rocky. It was very dry. Chantry saw no tracks but their own.

He looked around again. . . . Still nothing.

Owen Chantry mopped the sweat from his face. He wished again that he owned a hat. He had borrowed an old one from Kernohan for a few days, but it had been left in the house. His own hat had been lost when he was riding north.

It was growing hotter. A grasshopper flew up and winged away in the distance. Overhead, a vulture circled. Chantry took off his coat and put it over the saddle before him.

Finally they reached a cave, which was perfectly screened by trees. The old man chuckled, pleased with himself. "Cain't see this here place from hardly nowheres. You got to know it's here, or come right down the canyon to it. Indians used to stop here. We'll just set tight an' leave 'em hunt for us, an' come tomorry we'll get goin' afore light comes."

There was no talking. They ate, slept, rested, waited. From time to time Chantry or the old man slipped out from behind the screen of trees and went up the canyon or down, scouting, listening.

Late in the day, they were all lying quiet when they heard the drum of hoofs on the rocks above, then silence.

"Hell," they heard somebody say. "They'd never go down there! It's a trap!"

"Dammit," said somebody else, "they can't just disappear! They got to be around here somewhere."

"Did you see any tracks? I found some back yonder in the dust but they faded out. Anyway, they wouldn't come this way! Why, this here heads right out into open country, an' there'd be no place to hide! I figure they went to the high country up yonder, where they can see round the country."

Then the riders went away, and Chantry grounded his rifle. The sun slowly sank, tinting the peaks of the mountains with gold and crimson.

The old man went up the rocks. When he returned he shook his head. "No sign of 'em. Might's well have some coffee. Eat up, 'cause we got a round-about ride to the rampart."

The stars came out. The tiny glow of the fire was lost in the vast darkness. The air around the cave was damp from the waters of a spring and the grass around it. The horses were picketed near the spring where they could browse or drink as they chose.

Chantry went to where Kernohan lay. The flickering firelight shone on his gaunt cheeks and sunken eyes. "How are you?" he asked.

"All right. Feel mighty tired, but I don't hurt much."

"We've a long ride ahead."

"So I heard. Le's go on an' ride, Mr. Chantry. I'll not hold you back." He was silent for a few minutes, and Chantry sat on a slab fallen from the overhang and sipped his coffee. "That boy's doin' all right, ain't he?" asked Kernohan.

"He sure is. He's carrying his weight and more. You've no need to worry about him."

"I reckon. 'Though a body does worry. Times are hard for a boy his age. No young folks, no dances, socials or such. Why, he ain't seen a box supper since he was eight!"

"This is a beautiful country," said Chantry. "There will be people along soon, lots of them. There're a good many in the San Luis valley already, and just a few years ago a man named Baker led a party into the San Juans. We're just the first. Doby will have plenty of company soon."

At moonrise, they moved off with Chantry leading. He started at a rapid trot and held it. The trails were narrow, but they were plain to see in the moonlight.

The old man moved up beside Chantry. "You ride keerful, young feller. Them boys might be most anywheres about."

From time to time Chantry drew up, listening, trying the air for smoke. He doubted if the renegades were so far east, but they could be.

The night was cool and still, almost cold. The peaks were harsh against the blue black sky and bright stars. There was no sound but the creak of saddles and the fall of hoofs. Once Kernohan coughed. Owen Chantry looked ahead. The rifle felt good in his hands.

The old man dropped back to spell Doby at leading the packhorses, and the boy rode forward to join Chantry.

"Where you think they are?" Doby asked, low-voiced.

Chantry shrugged. "No telling, Doby."

The fire had gone out.

Mac Mowatt was hunched against a tree, chewing on a chunk of elk meat. He felt sour and old, and there was no pleasure in him.

Frank was gone. Pulled out. He'd never believed that Frank would leave him—although it was obvious he was discontented. Mac Mowatt was sore as an old grizzly with a bad tooth. He stared at Ollie Fenelon, who was rubbing his burned scalp, which was now beginning to peel. Then his eyes went to Pierce, at the fire.

Jake Strawn had drawn away from the others and was sitting by himself. Strawn was something of a loner, anyway. And tonight Mowatt was especially remembering what Chantry had advised. To get close to Strawn and keep him close.

How many of them could he trust? Mowatt knew the answer . . . probably not one of them, unless it was his own kinfolk, and he was none too sure about them. The losses they had taken, the wounded men, the man with the broken leg. They'd been out maneuvered by Chantry every time. It rankled. They'd spent too much time in these hills with nothing to show for it. And despite all his arguments, he knew some of the men were beginning to doubt there was anything here.

Frank was gone. Mac knew that some of them had set great store by Frank. He was solid. He was *there*, and you knew he was there. Strawn was just lingering on, and Tom Freka paid almost no attention to Mowatt's orders anymore.

They were a sorry bunch . . . a sorry bunch.

He lifted the coffee cup to his lips, and at that very moment he heard the horse. He saw Tom Freka come to his feet like a cat. Mowatt dropped his cup and got up fast.

Chantry had slowed his horse to let the old man come abreast. Doby had turned in his saddle to look for his father. And the next thing they knew they were right in the middle of the Mowatt camp.

The shock was complete on both sides. It was Freka who came to life first, leaping to his feet and grabbing for his gun. But Owen Chantry had quickly lunged his horse forward. The horse's shoulder hit Freka as his gun came up, and he was knocked sprawling into Strawn, who was just rising off the ground.

Wiley raised up, grabbing a rifle. Using his rifle in one hand like a pistol, Chantry thrust it at him and fired. Wiley gave a choking cry and fell backward, his arms and legs all spread out, his chest bloody. And then there was only a roar of sound, of guns and screams and yells, leaping men and charging horses. Mac Mowatt got off a shot, charged forward and then fell back just in time to escape being run over by the packhorses.

Then it was over.

It had been a wild, crazy two minutes of gunfire and screams. Then the gunfire was scattered, and clothes were burning, the coffee was spilled, and Mowatt's men were scrambling back around the burned out coals of their campfire.

The riders were gone. Freka, on his feet, was still grabbing about for his gun, dropped from his hand. When he found it, he turned and ran for his horse.

Mowatt swore and shouted orders. "Get your hosses an' git!" he yelled. "Get 'em, damn it! *Get 'em!*" . . . They followed his orders.

Strawn got up and brushed off his clothes. The others, save Mac Mowatt and Pierce, who was looking at their last shattered coffeepot, were already gone. Mac Mowatt had started for his own horse, then hesitated. After a moment he walked over and picked up his fallen cup. It was empty, and he swore.

"Let 'em go, Mac," Strawn suggested. "They won't find anything. And if they do, they'll wish they hadn't."

"You think they did it a-purpose?" Pierce asked.

"Uh-uh," Strawn said. "They come up on us by accident. Surprised them as much as us." He nodded to indicate Wiley's body. "You better have you a look. I figure he's dead. Owen Chantry don't miss very often."

Pierce crossed to the fallen man. "Dead, all right. Through the heart, looks like." He turned to Mac. "Let's get out of here. Next thing we know it'll be one of us."

"Get out?" Mowatt rumbled. "I'll be damned if I will! There's gold up there, I tell you! Gold!"

Jake Strawn glanced around. "And what if there is? How far do you think it would take you with this outfit? They'd murder you for what's in your pocket, most of 'em. I say we get out and stay out. And then, after awhile, we come back nice and quiet like, with only a few of us . . . the ones who can be trusted."

Pierce nodded. "I like that. I really do. Catch 'em off guard, an' by that time Chantry'll have the gold."

"Will they leave for good?" Mac Mowatt asked.

"They will . . . chances are, except for Freka. He wants Marny."

"*What?*" Mowatt's head came up. "Tom Freka? I'd kill him first!"

"You ain't noticed?" Strawn asked. "Well, I have. And the man's not normal. Not human. There's something wrong with him."

"I'll kill him," Mac Mowatt muttered.

"You may have to," Strawn said quietly. "You may just have to."

18 The cabin on the rampart lay still and cool under the dawn light. The sentinel pines stood straight and dark, austere as nuns at prayer. The leaves of the aspens trembled, and the high peaks of distant mountains were crowned with the gold of sunrise.

Their horses walked into the stillness, tired from the miles behind them, grateful for the scent of water and the end of their journey.

Owen Chantry dismounted and reached up to help Marny down, just a second before Doby reached her. Doby scowled and dropped his hands as if to imply that he had not even intended to help. Then he walked to his father, helped him from the saddle, and half-carried him into the house.

"Old man," Chantry said, "do you want to explore out there? Have a look around? You're probably the best scout among us."

"Maybe. Y'do pretty well your own self. Ain't

nothin' to fear from this place right here. A man could come up, but he'd make a powerful lot of noise gettin' through all that brush."

When the gear was stripped from the horses, the packs carried inside, and a bed made for Kernohan, Owen Chantry took his rifle and went out along the rim. The shadows were pulling back from the vast expanse to the west, where hundreds of miles of land lay open to the eye.

The land at the rim sloped off, then ended abruptly in a tremendous escarpment, a sheer wall of two hundred feet dropping away to talus slopes below.

Yet the cliffs were not smooth, but were fluted and broken. Suddenly, near the place where the walls of two escarpments met, he saw a narrow gap between a boulder and a raised portion of the wall. He peered through.

Here, hidden at the edge of the escarpment, was a secret place—a descent to the ground below, but an excellent firing position also. Several possible trails were in full view from here, and a man with a rifle—

"It shall be me," he said aloud. "Or the old man. Somebody who's good with a rifle."

Marny came up to meet him. "Can you see them?"

"They haven't found us yet."

"Have you found out where it is? I mean, whatever it is that's hidden?"

"I think I know how to find it now."

She looked out over the forest and meadows below. "It is beautiful. With all God's bounty, why must there be so much trouble?"

"That is the hardest question of history, Marny, the question people have asked in every age, in every time. Many men want what other men have. Men are often greedy, jealous, and vindictive. Or they look across the fence at what they think is greener grass. They pursue will-o'-the-wisp dreams, such as this 'treasure'."

Chantry scanned the horizon. Men have died, months of time have been wasted, and all to get something for nothing, to profit from someone else's spoils. And the end is not yet in sight."

"What will happen?" Marny looked up at him.

"They will come after us. They have committed themselves to a course of action. If they gave up now, all their efforts would go for nothing. So they will not give up."

"When will they come?"

"I don't know. But we must stop them . . . if we can."

"I hope that Mac Mowatt does not come with them. I wouldn't want to see him shot."

"Nor I."

Bright now was the land below, bright with the early sun, with the clearness of the sky.

It was a good land. Grazing land for the most part, but here and there a plain where something could grow well. A man could make a living here. And as mining increased—as it was bound to—he could sell beef cattle to the miners. And vegetables and grain also.

Chantry stooped and picked up a handful of the soil. Good . . . very good. . . . Many trees and plants grew here, and others could also grow. Down there on the flat, still others could grow. There was more water there. A man might choose crops by studying what already grew in the soil, and choosing those crops which needed the same soil, water, and climate.

He leaned on the rock and put his rifle beside him. His eyes again swept the vast green land that lay below. What a place Clive Chantry had chosen for his cabin! The rampart! There could not be a more beautiful view anywhere, nor one encompassing a wider lookout.

He was tired. The warm sun baked his muscles and he slowly relaxed.

"When this is over, Owen, where will you live?"

"Here. . . . If I'm alive. Or down there," he gestured below.

Then he saw them. Four riders in a small, neat group, coming out of a narrow draw near a canyon. They rode up out of the draw and came at a canter across a meadow, rode into the trees, then emerged again.

He pointed. "Marny? Look!"

She looked. They rode in a tight group, occasionally stringing out, then coming together again like figures in a square dance. "From here," she said quietly, "they look beautiful!"

"Yes," he agreed, watching them appear and disappear along the trail they followed.

"How far away are they?"

He shrugged. "A mile and a half. Two miles. They're slowing down now, and I think they're looking at us."

"You mean they see us?"

"No. They couldn't pick us out from here . . . I think they're scanning the wall for a way up."

"We'd better tell the others," Marny said.

"All right." But he hesitated, his eyes reaching out to the horizon. "There will be others, you know, coming by some other route."

"Do you want Doby?"

"No, tell him to check on his father, then locate the old man and work with him. They will have to cover the trail from the spring side. This may be a long fight, and it may be over quickly."

The riders below were closer now. Chantry caught the gleam of light from a rifle barrel. He watched them, and there were few places their trail led that could not be seen from his vantage point.

He tucked the rifle butt against his shoulder and lowered his cheek to the stock, sighting along the barrel, tracking them. They were too far away for a shot, but he was in no hurry. Nor had he any wish to waste his ammunition.

Suddenly, he was anxious. The riders must know they were up here. The riders must surely know that they could be seen. Then why . . . ?

He turned sharply and ran to the cabin.

He got to the door and saw Kernohan inside. He was sitting up in bed. "What's happened? What's wrong?" Kernohan asked him.

Kernohan's rifle was in a corner near the door, and Chantry caught it up with his left hand and threw it to the sick man. "We've got trouble," Chantry said.

He ducked away from the door and started for the trees. Suddenly a shadow loomed in the trees. He saw a rifle come up and then he shot from the hip. The bullet hit a tree near the man's face, scattering splinters and bark. Chantry worked the lever and fired again. The man's gun banged but no bullet sound followed. Chantry saw the man clinging to a tree, one arm around it. The man was staring at him with wide, empty eyes, his lips working with words that would not come out, that would never come out.

Owen Chantry ran past the dying man, catching up his rifle as he went. It was a Henry, and a good rifle. Suddenly he halted and went back to the man, now down on the ground, his shoulder and chest against the tree, his head hanging forward.

Without ceremony or hesitation, Chantry unbuckled his gun belt and jerked it free. There were twenty loops in the man's belt, all filled with .44s.

They had timed it nicely. The four horsemen below must have waited under cover until the others had circled around to come up to the house. While Chantry was watching the riders below, the men near the house had simply closed in. Luckily, he had guessed their strategy in time. Or had he?

There must be others. Where were they? Where was Marny? Where were the old man and Doby?

No sounds, no shots.

Was the man he had wounded or killed the only one near the house? He didn't think so. Where were the others?

He crouched behind a thick ponderosa at a point where another had fallen against it, offering a kind of cover.

A voice called out from somewhere in front of him. "Come on out, Chantry! Give yourself up! We've got the kid and we've got Marny Fox!"

"Is Mac Mowatt with you?" Chantry called back.

A momentary silence. Then: "No, he ain't. That ain't got nothing to do with it. You come out or we'll kill 'em both."

"I'd like to hear you say that to Mac Mowatt," he called back.

"You come on out. Throw down your guns and come on out."

Chantry eased his position, seeking a place to move, giving a glance to the ground cover to see how much noise he would make in moving. He thought he had the threatening voice located.

Where was the old man? Did Mowatt's gang even know about him?

"Come out, damn you, or we'll start busting the kid's fingers!"

"Who killed Clive?" Chantry asked, just loud enough to be heard. "I told you I wanted him . . . or them . . . hung. Have you done what I want?"

"Are you crazy? We're in command here!"

"Are you now?"

How many were there? Chantry was suddenly quite certain that there were no more than three, possibly two, and that if they *had* captured Doby and Marny, the boy and girl were not with these men.

He moved swiftly, silently, twenty yards in the trees and knelt down.

Where were Mowatt, Freka, and Strawn?

Chantry was poised for a move when he heard the sudden boom from a heavy rifle. There was a yell, then a volley of shots, then after a slight interval, the heavy boom again. Then swearing.

He crept toward the noise, carrying both rifles. Suddenly, he dropped his own rifle and threw the other to his shoulder. Several men had broken out of the brush and were running diagonally across from him. He opened fire. One man stumbled and fell, and another turned swiftly and levered three quick shots at Chantry. Something struck him a wicked blow and he fell. A second shot spat bark from the tree where his head had been just a moment ago. Chantry fired again but the men were gone.

He was on his knees, rising, when a man broke through the brush coming right straight at him. Chantry swung his rifle and caught him across the shins. The man's mouth opened in a scream, and Chantry left the ground in a lunging dive that knocked the man to the ground. The man tried to get up, swinging his gun to bring it to bear, and Chantry, lacking purchase or room for a proper swing, thudded the butt of his rifle against the man's chin.

Chantry himself staggered and fell against a tree.

The man, whoever he was, was out cold. Chantry threw the man's rifle into the trees and jerked off his gun belt. His left leg hurt bad, but he could see no blood.

Chantry decided to give up his spare rifle. It was too awkward to carry. He leaned it against a tree, half-hidden by low-growing branches.

Then he moved to another tree and limped into a thicker stand. Now he could see the corner of the cabin, some distance off through the forest. He had started toward it when his move was cut short.

"All right, Chantry! This is Strawn! Don't move!"

There was nothing else to do. Chantry stood perfectly still and they came up to him and took his gun.

19 A wrong move—a move of any kind, and he was dead. There was no nonsense about Strawn. He was not a vicious man, but he had killed and would kill again, and his shots were true.

To move was to die, and Owen Chantry was not ready to die.

"Looks like you win the hand, Jake," he said mildly. "I was hoping you weren't around."

"He's around, all right, and I am, too!" That would be Ollie Fenelon. Two more of the Mowatt men were coming up through the trees.

"Hell!" one of them exclaimed. "This ain't no buffalo gun! This here's a Henry!"

"Well? You heard it, didn't you? Sure sounded like a buffalo gun! Sounded like a big Sharps fifty! I'd a swore—"

"Mac wants to see you, Owen," Strawn said. "You just walk easy now and don't make me kill you."

Chantry had no choice but to follow.

When they came to Mowatt's camp, a fire was going, and Mac Mowatt was waiting for them.

"Well, Chantry," Mowatt was sitting, his heavy forearms locked about his knees. "You've given us some trouble. But now you're goin' to make it all worthwhile."

"Always glad to oblige," Chantry said, seating himself on a rock, "what can I do for you? Now, if you want to leave the country, you just take this trail along here—"

"Leave? Who said anythin' about leavin'?" Mowatt asked him.

"Well," Chantry said seriously, "it seems to me that if you want any of your men left, that's what you should do. I figured Strawn here took me because you needed a guide through the mountains, and there's nothing I'd rather do."

"Damn you, Chantry," Mowatt said. "Go to hell. All we want from you is treasure. Show us where it is and we'll let you go free."

Chantry smiled. "Now, Mac. Let's be honest. You'd never turn me loose. You know I'd only get another gun—"

Tom Freka had joined them. "Not without hands, you wouldn't. What if we took off your hands, Chantry? You got two hands now, but I got a bowie, an' Pierce has a ax to cut firewood."

"That sounds just like you, Freka," Chantry replied quietly. "You'd cut off my hands· because you know I can draw faster and shoot straighter than you. You're scared, Freka. You're just plain scared."

"Am I?" Freka took a big burning stick from the fire. "You also got two eyes. How would you like to try for ·one?"

"Put it down, Freka," Mowatt said. "I'll kill a man, but I'll be damned if I'll torture one."

"Then how do you expect us to find that treasure?" Freka asked. "You think he'll just up an' tell us?"

"Why not, Freka?" Chantry said. "Mowatt's a gentleman. And Strawn here's a man of his word. I'd trust either one of them." He stretched his stiff leg out before him. "Mowatt, do you have Marny and the boy . . . Doby?"

"I do. Catched 'em unexpected like. Yeah, I got 'em all. Back yonder."

Mowatt pointed back over his shoulder.

"Turn them loose. Let them get out of here with their horses and Doby's father, and I'll take you to whatever it is, if I can."

"You think we gonna believe *that?*" Freka demanded.

"I believe him, Freka," Strawn said.

Mowatt shifted his position and took out his pipe. "Figure it this way, Chantry. We got you. We got them. The boy's old man is mighty sick hurt. We ain't got to argue with nobody, an' we ain't got to deal with nobody. Either you tell us what we want, or we let that man die. We might even shoot Doby."

Mowatt drew on his pipe to test the stem, then began to tamp tobacco. "We might even kill you."

"You might. But I don't think you will," said Chantry. "Not if you know what's good for Marny."

"You don't seem to get the idea," Mowatt said. "You ain't in no position to bargain, Chantry. You got no place to stand. Just get us that treasure an' you'll have no more trouble."

"Release my friends," Chantry said quietly, "then hang the man who killed Clive, and I'll show you the treasure."

"You goin' to listen to that talk?" Freka snorted.

"Well, I don't know about that," Pierce Mowatt said. "It might be a right good deal."

"Might be at that," Jake Strawn said. "We got nothing against the boy, or his pa either."

"Chantry's a troublemaker," Freka said angrily. "Can't you see? He's tryin' to get us fightin' amongst ourselves."

"Seems to me," Chantry said, "that the killer should volunteer to be hung, just for the good of his friends."

He was smiling easily, but his mind was working swiftly.

"Where's the treasure, Chantry?" Mowatt asked bluntly.

"You boys have kept me so busy I haven't had time to look." Chantry shrugged.

They had his gun, and they had his rifle, but somewhere not half a mile away the captured rifle still leaned against a tree.

"Chantry," Mowatt spoke slowly and carefully, "I want you to get this straight. You've given us a sight of trouble, an' we ain't goin' to put up with it. You got you one more chance. Find whatever it was Clive Chantry brought out of Mexico. If you don't, I'll not leave you to the boys. I'll shoot you myself."

"Looks like I don't have much choice," Chantry said. "But all I've got is a clue."

"What's the clue?" Pierce demanded.

"I know what the clue is," Chantry admitted, "but I don't know how to read it. Like it or not, I'm going to need time.

"When Clive was murdered, he wasn't quite dead when he was left behind. So he left me something to work on."

"What could he leave if he was dyin'?" It was Freka again.

"He wrote something on the door step. He wrote the word ten."

They stared at him.

"Ten? What's that mean?" Freka demanded. "Ten what?"

"My thought exactly, gentlemen," Chantry said. "Ten what? Then I wondered, if it was ten feet, ten miles, ten inches, then why didn't he write the numeral? Why the word *ten*?"

"Don't make no sense," Ollie Fenelon muttered. "It surely don't."

"You figgered it out yet?" Mowatt asked.

"Maybe. I think he was trying to write *Tennyson*." Chantry said.

"Tennyson? What's that?" Pierce demanded.

"It ain't what," Mowatt said. "It's *who*. It's a man's name."

"Name of who?" Ollie asked. "I never heard such a name."

"It's a writer," Mowatt said. He glared around at the others. "If you would *read* once in awhile you'd know somethin'. Tennyson is a writer." He glanced at Chantry. "English ain't he?"

"English . . . and a poet. A very good poet."

"Poet?" Ollie was shocked. "What would a man write a poet's name for when he was dyin'?"

"I like his poetry," Chantry said quietly. "And so did Clive. Whatever he'd hidden he didn't wish anyone to find it but me. So he was trying to conceal it in such a way that only I *could* find it."

"Hell!" Freka spat. "If one man can find it, another man can too."

"You've tried, I think," Chantry said. "But what have you found? You're welcome to go on trying. There's room enough for every one to look. Be my guest."

"If you know something sure, stop talkin' so much an' tell us," Mowatt said. "Was it somethin' in one o' them books he left?"

"Of course." Chantry got to his feet and stretched. Three guns were on him, and the men who held those guns were ready to kill him. But not quite yet. They wanted to know what he knew.

"We both liked Tennyson," Chantry said. "Certain of Tennyson's poems we both liked very much, so Clive naturally thought of something he knew I would think of also. The secret to the hiding place is hidden in one of Tennyson's poems."

"In a poem! Who'd a thought of that?" Fenelon was disgusted. But suddenly his mood changed. "I don't believe it! I don't believe one cottonpickin' word. You made the whole thing up!"

"Maybe some of it," Strawn said, "but I seen that *ten.* Never paid it no mind."

Mac Mowatt was watching Chantry with careful eyes. "All right, what next?" he asked finally.

"I'll need a copy of Tennyson," Chantry said.

"You sure?" Mowatt stared at him, eyes hard. "Don't you *remember?* Didn't you learn it by heart?"

"No," said Chantry, "I didn't. I don't even know which poem it's in. I'll need the book, and I'll need some time to study it at the cabin."

"We ain't got no time to waste," said Freka.

"We'll all go along." Mowatt said. "All but Whitey and Slim. Just so's the rest of us stay together. Wouldn't want nothin' to go wrong now."

Under his breath, Chantry swore. His mouth was dry, the taste bitter. This was his last chance.

20 "You're not gonna need us all," Freka said, "I'll just stay here with Whitey and Slim and the prisoners."

"You'll come with us," Mowatt said sternly.

Tom Freka got to his feet slowly and he spat into the fire. "Whitey can stay," he said, "but I'll stay, too."

Owen Chantry felt his muscles slowly relax, yet all his senses were alert. This might be a showdown, and if—

"All right, Tom," Mowatt was suddenly easy. "Maybe you're just wore out. You set by while the rest of us pick up that gold. You just set by." He let his eyes shift to Whitey, a hard-faced man. "Whitey, I'm holdin' you responsible for the people I'm leavin'. That goes for all of 'em. They're not to be hurt, y'understand?"

Whitey nodded. "I hear you, Mowatt. They won't be."

Mowatt led the men off. When they were out of earshot of the camp, Pierce suggested, "Maybe I should go back?"

"They'll be all right," Mowatt said.

"I wouldn't leave any woman where Freka is," Chantry said.

"Ain't none of your damn business, Chantry," Mowatt told him roughly. "Just lead us to that treasure now."

They walked the distance to the cabin.

Chantry stopped in the clearing just shy of the cabin. A gun prodded his back.

"What y' stoppin' for?" Pierce demanded.

Chantry didn't answer.

"All right, get goin'," Mowatt said.

Chantry walked forward, and seeing the door partially open, he pushed it gently with his hand. The door swung inward.

The room was empty, the bed was made. A few coals were gleaming in the fireplace. A blackened pot on the hearth steamed slowly. Chantry glanced quickly around. He saw no gun, nothing he could use for a weapon. He felt like he'd been struck in the belly. He had hoped . . . he scarcely knew any longer what he had hoped.

Mowatt pushed him hard from behind, and he staggered. "Damnit, get in there!" Mowatt shoved in after him, glaring around.

The books were on the table where he'd put them.

Chantry glanced out of the north window. Like the south window, it was small, almost like a porthole, though somewhat larger. It was rounded at the top.

"Now look at them books!" Mowatt said. "And you better find somethin' quick!"

Mowatt took up the books one by one and riffled their pages.

At one point a torn scrap of paper had been used for a bookmark. It was at the poem, "Ulysses." Mowatt read the poem slowly, his lips moving, occasionally scowling over some word or meaning. "Hell," he said, at last, "there ain't nothing there!"

Only there was.

He offered Chantry the book. Chantry made a show of turning the pages as if searching for a clue. Ollie Fenelon and Pierce Mowatt went outside, and he could hear them muttering over "Stuff an' nonsense."

Chantry knew that "Ulysses" had been a special favorite of Clive's. They had quoted it to each other in letters and written of certain passages in it.

One passage that Chantry especially remembered began: "Yet all experience is an arch wherethrou'/ Gleams that untravell'd world whose margin fades/ For ever and for ever when I move."

Reading quickly from first one poem and then another Chantry paced the floor.

Pausing in his pacing, he looked out of the north window. Only trees in a dense stand beyond an area of rock, scattered shrubs and young aspens.

Yet the top of the window could be called an arch. He went back to turning the pages.

Chantry sat down on the edge of the bed. "Damn it," he muttered, with a great show of irritation, "it's got to be here."

"It better be," Mowatt said.

Again Chantry paced the floor. This time he stopped in the middle of the room, reading a couple of lines from "Locksley Hall" aloud as though searching for something in them. Then he looked out through the south window.

The sky was a brilliant blue. The sun shone brightly. A big granite rock was visible above the green of the grass.

Chantry had started to turn away when something flashed across his vision . . . a faint gleam. He took his eyes from the window and slowly turned a page.

"What was you lookin' at then?" Mowatt demanded.

"I was just thinking," Chantry replied. "Clive was never a simple man. I've got to put myself in his shoes and try to think like him. I may seem to be daydreaming, but I'm not."

Mac Mowatt hitched around in his chair. "Your funeral," he said shortly. "But I'm gettin' mighty impatient. And so are the boys."

"You haven't yet hung the killer of my brother," Chantry said. "And I gave your men two weeks."

Mowatt came off his chair with a lunge and backhanded Chantry across the mouth. He staggered, falling against the wall. Instantly, the men outside were in the doorway.

Mowatt waved a hand. "It's all right. He just gave me some lip. You boys relax. I can handle this."

Mowatt sat down again and Chantry picked up the fallen book. He tasted blood, and his lip was swelling where it had smashed against his teeth.

"You keep a still tongue now," said Mowatt. "I got no time to waste."

Chantry lifted his eyes to the window. There, by the big granite rock where the secret way went down the mountain, there was a gleam . . . a bit of mica in the rock reflecting light. Chantry turned his eyes away and knew what he intended to do. It was a long, long chance to take, and it meant some close-up shooting, and a chance that he'd be killed.

He smiled.

"What you smilin' at?" Mowatt demanded.

Chantry continued to smile. "I was just thinking of your faces when I find it," he said, "because I know it isn't what you think. You've been a fool, Mowatt, leading your men on a wild-goose chase, getting several of them killed, and several hurt. And all for nothing."

Chantry wanted him close. He wanted him to hit again. He had to get him close.

"I was smiling, too," he added, "to think how foolish we all are. Everybody dies sometime. The one thing we know about life is that we never get out alive, so why not live like a proud man? Mowatt, you're a yellow-bellied coward to hit an unarmed man. You are no gentleman, not even a shadow of one. You're leading a murdering, cowardly band of renegades, and not one of them would stand up to a man in a fair fight.

"And you, Mac Mowatt, supposed to be a fearless leader. I heard you back up for Freka . . . afraid to face him down. You're nothing, Mowatt, nothing at all. You haven't the guts of a mouse."

Chantry was ready, poised for attack, but it didn't come. Mac Mowatt leaned back in his chair and grinned at him, his eyes cold and crafty.

"You talk a lot, Chantry," he said, "but you ain't got what it takes. I know just what you're thinkin'. Like I'll get mad, jump you, you'll try for my gun, an' then you'll shoot it out. Well, it ain't a-gonna work.

"Oh, I'm mad, all right! As for Freka, I'll handle him my own way, and I need no help from you. Meanwhile, you got you one minute. You tell me where that gold is." Mowatt drew his gun and balanced it in his palm, muzzle upward.

"Read it," growled Mowatt.

" 'Yet all experience is an arch wherethrou'/Gleams that untravell'd world whose margin fades/For ever and for ever when I move.' "

"Don't mean nothin' to me," Mowatt said. The gun was steady in his hand, its muzzle lined on Chantry's chest.

"Look, Mowatt. The window is the arch. And looking out the window, you can see the sun reflecting off the mica. That's the gleam. If you shift your head a mite, the gleam fades and you lose it. That's 'whose margin fades/For ever and for ever when I move.' "

"Thanks, Chantry." Mac Mowatt was smiling. "Now you've given me all I need."

He eared back the hammer on his gun.

What was happenin' to 'em I couldn't find out. All I knew was that if me an' Marny was to get out of this alive I surely had to do somethin', an' fast.

Whitey was a tough, mean man, an' nobody to tangle with if it could be avoided, and there he set behind a slab of pine he'd picked up from a lightnin'-blasted tree, a-playin' solitaire with a greasy deck of cards. He sat there facin' us where we could never move without his seein', his cards in his hands, his six-shooter lyin' on the slab right there beside him.

Slim had come back and was watching Whitey's game an' I happened to glance up an' seen something wavin' at me. It was a hand, and it was that old man.

He was in the edge of the woods and he had that ol' buffalo gun and he was kind of gesturin', seemed to me, toward Slim and then himself.

It taken me no time to see what he meant. He was going to take Slim and that left Whitey for me. Well, he sure picked the easy one. Tacklin' that Whitey was like jumping right down a grizzly's throat, but I aimed to do it.

I reached over an' taken Marny's wrist and kinda squeezed, puttin' my feet back for a quick getup as I done it, so she'd know somethin' was up. First time I ever touched her.

That old coon hunter out there, he taken aim with that ol' buffalo gun and I looked up at Slim just a minute, an' I couldn't help but say it. I said, "Goodbye, Slim," and his eyes come to mine, and then that gun boomed.

What the buffalo gun done to him, I never seen, 'cause when it boomed I left the ground in a lunge, and I swung one from the hip that clobbered Whitey right in the face. He went over backward, grabbin' for his gun that was falling off the slab, and Slim, he was on the ground near me, kickin' an' squawlin'.

Whitey come off the ground but I swung another fist into him and the gun somehow landed near my feet. I ducked an' grabbed for it, but Whitey kicked me in the head, knockin' me back to the ground. And then I heard a gun go off close up, and I was certain I was shot.

When I opened my eyes and started to get up, Marny was standin' there with a gun in her hand an' Whitey was dead.

Then something slammed into my skull, I heard a scream an' another gunshot, and then I was rolling in the dust and branches from a fallen tree an' my head was roaring with sound an' a stabbing pain. I fought to get up. Got up, staggered, and scraped my palms on tree bark when I tried to hold myself from fallin' again.

Blood was streamin' into my eyes and all I could see was Tom Freka up on a horse. He had Marny and she was unconscious, seemed like, and they were ridin' away through the trees.

Whitey was on the ground where Marny had shot him to save me, and I jumped for him, trying to find the gun Marny must have dropped near him. I found it and came up holding it.

Then a man I never seen before come running at me. He skidded to a halt when he seen me and he says, "Drop it, kid, or I'll kill you!" and I shot him right through the brisket.

21 Chantry had no faith in the breaks, but he knew one when he saw it.

The hammer on Mac Mowatt's gun eared back and from somewhere outside a buffalo gun boomed. The boom of that big gun, unexpected as it was, froze Mac Mowatt for one instant. Chantry needed no more.

He swung a long-stretched kick at the tilted-up leg of Mowatt's chair and hooked it. The chair went over and Mowatt with it. And the gun went off into the ceiling.

Chantry threw the Tennyson at him and followed it in, and as Mowatt floundered in the tangle of book and chair, he kicked him in the belly and wrenched the gun from his hand. He heard the snap of a bullet past his ear and the thud of it into the wall, and then he fired. Mowatt lay still.

His next bullet caught Ollie Fenelon filling the doorway and a second one hit Ollie as he fell into the room, Ollie's gun falling from his hand. Snatching Ollie's gun, Chantry jumped for the door: Pierce Mowatt had a rifle and it was lifting as Chantry stepped into the door and chopped down on him with both guns. Pierce took a step back and fell, tried to get up and then lay still.

And there, across a small clearing, his six-shooter in its holster, stood Jake Strawn.

"Chantry, take my horse," he said, "Tom Freka's prob'ly got your girl."

That big blood bay was standing there, saddled for traveling, and Chantry swung into the saddle. "Thanks!" he yelled, and then the bay was running.

Jake Strawn had need of a fast horse from time to time, and this was the horse that could outrun anything in the country.

Chantry had heard some gunshots from far away and feared the worst.

Doby was at the Mowatt camp, standing all spraddle-legged, only half aware of what was happening. There was blood all over his head and two men down. Doby yelled and pointed out the direction, and the bay began to run again.

Freka's tracks were fresh, and the bay seemed to know that was where they were going.

The trail was narrow, and the slender stems of aspens bent over the trail in arches, like the crossed swords at a military wedding. It was like riding down a tunnel, only there was dust in Chantry's nostrils until they broke into open meadow.

Not knowing the country, Freka had been riding blind and, in his haste, had reached a dead end.

He was seeking a trail out when he saw the big bay, believing its rider to be Strawn. "Lay off, Jake!" Freka shouted. "This gal is mine!"

Then he saw it was Chantry, and his face went white. He let go of Marny, who slid from the saddle to the ground. Freka's horse stepped away from the fallen girl, and Freka snarled, "How'd you get that horse Chantry?"

"Jake let me have him, Freka. He said you had my girl."

"Never knowed she was yours," Tom said, "or I'd a taken her sooner. I see you got a drawn gun. That gives you a edge."

"You never had an edge, Freka?" Chantry was relentless. Marny was stirring. She was going to get up, and he wished she would stay where she was.

"I didn't think the almighty Owen Chantry needed a edge. You holster your gun an' I'll beat you."

"You might . . . and you might not. But I'm not aiming to give you a break. You're a woman-killing snake."

Chantry dropped his gun into its holster. He saw Freka's hand move to cover him. His hand already just above his own gun, Chantry simply brought it out again and fired.

Freka had white pearl button's on his dark blue shirt. The button on his left pocket flap vanished and was replaced by crimson.

Chantry walked the big bay closer as Freka tried to bring his suddenly too heavy gun to bear. "I'm not a woman, Freka," he said. "You should have stuck to killing women."

There was no need to waste another bullet. The gun slid from Freka's fingers and he slumped in the saddle, still holding the reins and looking at Owen Chantry with staring eyes.

"He let you have that horse. I never knowed him to—"

"Jake Strawn is a man, Freka. A bad man, but a man."

Freka fell from his horse, his boot hanging in the stirrup. The horse walked off a few steps, dragging Freka face down in the dirt.

Owen Chantry rode the bay over, disengaged Freka's boot, and let his leg fall. Then he rode back to Marny Fox, leading Freka's horse behind him.

"We'd better go back," he said gently. "They'll be worried."

When Marny rode in with Chantry beside her, Strawn was waiting near the cabin. Chantry swung down. "Thanks, Jake. Lucky you had him saddled."

"Glad to oblige, Chantry," Strawn said, "I've had enough of Mowatt's crew. Them that's still alive has scattered. I figgered I'd ride down El Paso way and see Frank."

"Frank's a good man, Jake. One of the best."

Jake Strawn mounted his bay, then turned in the saddle. "How'd it go, Owen? With Freka, I mean?"

"He won't kill anymore," said Chantry.

"He was the one killed Clive," said Strawn.

"That's what I guessed," said Chantry. "But much obliged. I'm happy to know for sure."

Strawn started to ride away.

"Jake?"

He pulled up. "If you ever want to sell that horse—?"

"Not a chance!" Jake replied, and rode away.

Chantry looked slowly around. Kernohan, looking pale and weak but on his own feet, came in from the aspens. Doby was with him, and the old man—looking even grayer now and leaning on his Buffalo gun as he walked.

"Is it over, Owen?"

"I think so, Doby." Chantry smiled. It felt like his first smile in months. "Except for burying the dead and finding the treasure. How'd you like to find the treasure?"

"Now?" Doby asked.

"Now," said Chantry. And slowly he led the way to the boulder, followed by Marny, Kernohan, and Doby.

The foot of the boulder where the hidden trail went steeply down offered a splendid view. Chantry paused there for a moment, drinking in the magnificence of it.

Clive had sighted well. Close up, the bit of mica was hard to find. Chantry stepped back and looked thoughtfully at the rock, then studied to the right and left of it. Finally, he stepped into the cleft and began a close examination of the rock.

Once he found it, the hiding place seemed obvious and scarcely could be termed anything of the kind. More than likely, Clive's only thought had been to put it away from the danger of fire, always something to be reckoned with in cabins with open hearths.

It was just a little hole in the boulder, the opening blocked off by a rock. After displacing the rock, Chantry removed a rusted metal box. He broke it open. Inside was a roll of parchment covering a sheaf of papers. The parchment was wrapped in oilskin.

Doby leaned over and peered into the hole, then at the now empty box. "Is that treasure?" he asked.

Carefully, without answering, Owen Chantry removed the oilskin cover and gently unrolled the parchment. It was a deep tan in color and written upon with firm and elegant handwriting: *"This manuscript to be delivered to my friend Jean Jacques Tremoulin, Paris, France. The Legends of the Otomi as Collected by Clive Chantry."*

Chantry read the words aloud. They stared at the manuscript in wonder, as Chantry turned the oilskin inside out. When he did so, a tiny gold nugget slipped free and fell to the ground.

Doby was struck with awe. He'd never seen real gold before, but he knew what it was.

Treasure . . . gold . . . and value. . . .

It was a whole lot to understand at once, Chantry knew, especially for a poor country boy.

"Anyway," said Chantry, "we're going to be neighbors now. The war is over." He reached for Marny's hand.

For war it had been.

"I'm mighty glad," said Kernohan. "Us down there and you up here. You're a mighty generous man, Chantry." He was weak on his feet, but he could walk.

"And you must visit us often, Doby," said Marny, "being as close by as you are."

Doby grinned. She was a little too old for him anyway. One of these days, he'd just take him a trip to El Paso.

In the stillness of a mountain grove high above,

the old man looked down at the people, dead and alive.

He'd helped. He'd taken his shots, and made them when they counted, *where* they counted.

Enclosed by the silence around him, broken only by a bird call, the old man bent down, drank from a small stream, and wiped his mouth.

"The trouble with people is," he said, aloud to himself, "they make too damn much noise!"

ABOUT THE AUTHOR

LOUIS L'AMOUR, born Louis Dearborn L'Amour, is of French-Irish descent. Although Mr. L'Amour claims his writing began as a "spur-of-the-moment thing," prompted by friends who relished his verbal tales of the West, he comes by his talent honestly. A frontiersman by heritage (his grandfather was scalped by the Sioux), and a universal man by experience, Louis L'Amour lives the life of his fictional heroes. Since leaving his native Jamestown, North Dakota, at the age of fifteen, he's been a longshoreman, lumberjack, elephant handler, hay shocker, flume builder, fruit picker, and an officer on tank destroyers during World War II. And he's written four hundred short stories and over fifty books (including a volume of poetry).

Mr. L'Amour has lectured widely, traveled the West thoroughly, studied archaeology, compiled biographies of over one thousand Western gunfighters, and read prodigiously (his library holds more than two thousand volumes). And he's watched thirty-one of his westerns as movies. He's circled the world on a freighter, mined in the West, sailed a dhow on the Red Sea, been shipwrecked in the West Indies, stranded in the Mojave Desert. He's won fifty-one of fifty-nine fights as a professional boxer and pinch-hit for Dorothy Kilgallen when she was on vacation from her column. Since 1816, thirty-three members of his family have been writers. And, he says, "I could sit in the middle of Sunset Boulevard and write with my typewriter on my knees; temperamental I am not."

Mr. L'Amour is re-creating an 1865 Western town, christened Shalako, where the borders of Utah, Arizona, New Mexico, and Colorado meet. Historically authentic from whistle to well, it will be a live, operating town, as well as a movie location and tourist attraction.

Mr. L'Amour now lives in Los Angeles with his wife Kathy, who helps with the enormous amount of research he does for his books. Soon, Mr. L'Amour hopes, the children (Beau and Angelique) will be helping too.

BANTAM'S #1
ALL-TIME BESTSELLING AUTHOR
AMERICA'S FAVORITE WESTERN WRITER

- ☐ CATLOW   2037 $1.25
- ☐ DOWN THE LONG HILLS   2038 $1.25
- ☐ THE FIRST FAST DRAW   2064 $1.25
- ☐ THE MAN CALLED NOON   2083 $1.25
- ☐ NORTH TO THE RAILS   2087 $1.25
- ☐ HIGH LONESOME   2132 $1.25
- ☐ THE HIGH GRADERS   2138 $1.25
- ☐ CHANCY   2201 $1.25
- ☐ THE SACKETT BRAND   2235 $1.25
- ☐ FALLON   2313 $1.25
- ☐ THE MAN FROM THE BROKEN HILLS   2377 $1.25
- ☐ FLINT   2386 $1.25
- ☐ THE FERGUSON RIFLE   2388 $1.25
- ☐ THE DAY BREAKERS   2473 $1.25
- ☐ REILLY'S LUCK   6445 $1.25
- ☐ KIOWA TRAIL   6643 $1.25
- ☐ RIVERS WEST   7940 $1.25
- ☐ SACKETT'S LAND   8781 $1.25

Buy them at your local bookstore or use this handy coupon for ordering: